A GiRL called T.O.M.

Granny For Sale

Jackie Marchant

ILLUSTRATED BY LORETTA SCHAUER

WACKY BEE

Chapter 1

It's true. I really did try to sell my grandmother. Before I explain why, let me tell you something about her.

Granny likes travelling. Unfortunately, whenever she goes on one of her trips, she comes back with something *special* for my brother and me. Last time her special present was a lump of **DRIED-UP POO**. Not any old poo – this was rare poo from an endangered breed of large animal and she was helping out by buying its **POO**.

A GIRL called T.O.M.

While my brother went off to inspect his poo under his microscope, I tried to flush mine down the loo. You wouldn't believe how hard it is to flush rare breed poo down the loo. **IT FLOATED.** Three times I tried, until Dad was pounding on the door asking me What I Was Doing in There. I couldn't leave it in case he thought I'd done it, so I stuffed the soggy **POO** up my tee-shirt and left the bathroom with an innocent smile. Then I hid the **POO** in the bottom corner of the bin.

But Granny found the **POO** and I had to have a long talk about Being Grateful. The talk was delivered by Dad, who was dressed up as **DARTH VADER** (I'll explain later). But his cloak was too long and he kept standing on it, while his voice simulator kept breaking down and making him

6

squeak. I did my best to look ashamed, but that's quite hard when you're trying not to laugh.

Then, something truly awful happened – my teacher Mr Truber asked Granny to come into school and tell my class all about her trip.

The problem is, Granny doesn't tell. She acts. That means flapping her arms about and doing her voices, everything from screech to loud whisper. But the worst thing is, she thinks she's being funny. That's because the whole class is laughing – apart from me. I'm the girl with her eyes screwed shut, wishing that her dad's invisibility cloak really worked and she'd remembered to bring it to school.

'Where's my lovely Tom-Tom girl?' Granny looks around the class until her eyes settle on the poor girl trying to hide under a desk – me.

A GIRL called T.O.M.

Tom-Tom girl. That's what she calls me. Because my name is Tom. I should probably explain why I'm a girl called Tom.

It started with my brother. According to Granny, it is tradition in her family for a grandmother to name her first grandchild (I don't know which side of the family this came from – she probably made it up). Granny was hoping for a girl and was going to call her Andromeda. But when my brother was born she decided she couldn't call a boy Andromeda, so she called him ℋEAVENLY instead. It's short for My ℋEAVENLY ℬOY.

We just call him ℋEAVEN.

After that, Dad insisted on naming me. He named me Thora Odina, which is long for Thor Odin – after the **SUPERHERO**, not the Norse god. Dad changed his surname from Malik to Marvel long before he met my mum, so my name is Thora Odina Marvel.

Put my initials together and you get Tom. That's me – a girl called Tom.

But back to the **POO**. Back to the memory of Granny dragging me out from under the desk, where I'm trying to hide and pretend I've never seen her before. She then makes me hold the **POO** up for everyone to see. When she realises that it's gone out of shape, she squeezes it back again, by which time even Mr Truber has tears of laughter streaming down his face.

A GIRL called T.O.M.

Did I mention that the **POO** was supposed to be carved into the shape of the rare animal it came from? I don't know what animal exactly, but after being flushed three times and flung into the bin, it's not surprising it looked more like a lump of **POO**. Which is what it was.

That was last term, and some kids still call me Poo-girl.

But this wasn't why I wanted to sell Granny. That was something far worse.

Chapter 2

The trouble began the day Dad collected us from school dressed as **WONDER WOMAN**. By *us* I mean me, Narinda, and the twins. Narinda is my best friend and her parents have the shop next to ours. The twins are Lem and Kap and their mum has the shop the other side of ours, at the end of **Pickford Parade**. The twins are a year below, as wild as their flaming red hair, and NOT my best friends.

'Hurry, Tom!' Dad sped across the playground, long wig and shiny blue cloak flowing behind him.

A GIRL called T.O.M.

'Spiderman has been captured by a giant octopus!' he panted. 'I have to rescue him or the world is doomed!'

You may have guessed that my dad is into **SUPERHEROES**. In fact, he makes a living out of it.

A GIRL called T.O.M.

He has a shop called **SUPERHERO** that sells costumes, masks, DVDs, comics, games, figurines, tee-shirts, watches, and anything you could think of. He also buys and sells **SUPERHERO** items on **E-SELLALOT**, which is an online auction site where you can sell odd stuff that people couldn't possibly want to buy, but do.

Dad also does re-enactment. That means he dresses up and acts out **SUPERHERO** stories, made up by him. That is why **WONDER WOMAN** could try to save **SPIDERMAN**, even though they never met in real life. I think the giant octopus is made up.

Believe it or not, there are adults out there who pay my dad to dress up in his costumes and act out stories. Sometimes they use the space behind the shop. Other times he hires Pickford Memorial Hall.

A GIRL called T.O.M.

I should probably tell you right now that I am not into **SUPERHEROES**. I prefer reality. In fact, if there were a **SUPERHERO** called *Normal Girl*, that would be me.

When he collected us dressed as **WONDER WOMAN**, Dad was on his way to Pickford Memorial Hall to rescue Spiderman before it was time for the Scouts to use it.

'Are you taking us home first?' I asked him. This was a good question. Many a time, I've had to go with him and help – normally by cleaning up after them before the Scouts arrive. You wouldn't believe how messy saving the world can be.

'There is no choice,' he said, adjusting his tights. 'I left my Lasso of Truth on the kitchen table. Then I have to pick **BATMAN** and **THOR** up – I'm going to need their help. 'Now get in the **WONDER CAR**. I've parked on a double yellow line.'

'Shouldn't we wait for the others?'

'Others?' said Dad, hitching up his **WONDER WOMAN** knickers, which were a bit loose on him. 'The world is in danger – wouldn't it be better to sacrifice three children to save it?'

'No,' I said, looking around for Narinda. She was chatting to Elsa, who's in our class. 'Anyway, here's Narinda.' She came over when she saw me frantically waving.

'Hello, Narinda,' said Dad. 'Tom will explain everything while I prepare the **WONDER CAR** for a speedy exit.' He swirled his shiny blue cloak and ran off, dodging his way through the parents and kids who'd come to stare.

'Saving the world again?' asked Narinda.

A GIRL called T.O.M.

'As soon as we've got the twins.'

'Good luck,' she said, pointing to where the two boys were fiercely tackling each other for their softball. Lem won and kicked it across the playground. It landed in front of Dad and nearly tripped him up.

'Can we have our ball back?' asked Kap.

'No time,' said Dad. 'Get in the car – quick!' He ran off with the muddy softball tucked under his cloak.

'Give it back!' They chased after him.

'First one there sits in the front!' yelled Lem. They were fighting by the time they reached the car.

'Come on, boys,' said Dad. 'What will **SPIDERMAN** think when I tell him I'm too late to save him because of a couple of fighting boys?'

'He'll be dead, won't he?' said Lem.

'Both of you, in the back,' ordered Dad. The boys did what **WONDER WOMAN** told them. Narinda went in the front and I sat between the boys. Dad pulled away with a screech of tyres that had mums glaring at him, dads waving, and kids cheering. We clung on all the way home, where Dad swerved into a tiny parking space outside the front of our shop, leaving the back end of the **WONDER CAR** sticking out.

I should probably tell you that the **WONDER CAR** is in fact a very large old American car, bright silver with a dangly sign in the back window that says:

SUPERHERO ON BOARD!!
If you want one of these for your car, you can buy them from our shop.

A GIRL called T.O.M.

It's not always called the **WONDER CAR**. Amongst other things, it's been called the **Batmobile**, the **Tardis,** and the **Starship Enterprise**, depending on which particular story Dad is making up. The car is always kept outside our shop, to attract customers. I wish he had a normal car and parked it round the back like Narinda's parents.

The boys jumped out of the car and ran round the back of their shop, punching each other. Narinda climbed out and thanked **WONDER WOMAN** for bringing her home from school, while my mum came rushing out of our shop waving a carrier bag.

'Your Lasso of Truth's in here,' she said. 'Will you be home for dinner?'

'Depends on the traffic.' Dad drove off with a

A GIRL called T.O.M.

squeal of tyres, to collect **BATMAN** and **THOR** (not the one I was named after – a man who pays my dad to dress up and play *SUPERHERO* games. His real name is Trevor.)

That's when I noticed something odd.

Chapter 3

I should have realised something was going on that morning. But everything seemed perfectly normal. Normal for my family, that is.

My **STAR TREK** alarm clock woke me up, demanding that I save the Starship Enterprise – in Klingon. [In case you don't know, the Starship Enterprise is from **STAR TREK**. Captain Kirk was its first captain and the Klingons were his deadly enemy.]

I speak Klingon. Not because I think it's cool, but

A GIRL called T.O.M.

because Dad teaches Klingon and sometimes it's only me and my brother in his class. The **STAR TREK** alarm clock was a birthday present and came from a box full of unsold ones. This one now lives on the shelf by my top bunk, next to a **BATMAN** and a **HULK** figurine that Dad gave me for my birthday – he told me they are priceless.

Breakfast was normal. **HEAVEN** went on and on about quantum physics or something, while Mum did her yoga humming. Dad was panicking about his **WONDER WOMAN** knickers, and I was sitting quietly waiting for my chocolate cereal milk to go the perfect shade of brown.

Mum stopped humming. 'Tom, how would you like to share **HEAVEN'S** room with him?'

Mum often says strange things when she's been humming. I think it's because her thoughts haven't quite fully formed and aren't ready to come out. I call them her motherisms.

The thing is, ℋEAVEN doesn't have what you'd call a room. What he has is four walls, a window, and a door. It has a floor and a ceiling (sort of). It contains several broken electronic items he thinks he can fix, fixed items waiting to be broken so he can fix them, a ceiling completely hidden by models of the solar system and other galaxies dangling from it, a telescope, a microscope, specimens lining up to go under the microscope, jars of things I'd rather not think about, a stack of books so high it's always falling over, boxes of experiments (don't ask), a game console that he made himself, things that **flash**, things that **FIZZ**, things that go bang, a whiteboard with maths all over it, a whiteboard with scribbles all over it, and a giant Jabba the Hutt.

A GIRL called T.O.M.

The thing is, you can't actually get into HEAVEN'S room. There is only space for one person at a time, and only HEAVEN knows how to go about his room without treading on something that goes **FIZZ** or **bang**. I think there is a bed in there, but you can't see it. He does have a wardrobe – at least, he has a couple of open doors with a pile of clothes hanging over them.

So, when Mum asked me if I'd like to share HEAVEN'S room with him, you can see why I thought it was a motherism.

There are two ways of answering motherisms. You either say I think so. Or you say I don't think so.

You can probably guess what I said.

'I don't think so.' HEAVEN spoke at the same time.

'Mmm,' said Mum. 'You're probably right.'

My milk had gone just the right shade of brown, so I thought no more of it. I went to school and Dad collected us dressed as **WONDER WOMAN**. Mum rushed out to give him the Lasso of Truth before Dad sped off to save the world.

That was when I noticed the bin liners. Two of

them, bulging with stuff, sitting on the pavement outside our shop. You might wonder why I thought this was odd but, the thing is, my family never throws anything away. It may turn out to be valuable, it has happy memories, it will go on **E-SELLALOT** when Dad gets round to it, etc etc. That is why our flat is only one step away from being as messy as HEAVEN'S room. My room is the only one that is vaguely tidy.

I have only ever seen bin liners outside our shop once, long ago when Mum and Dad cleared out the room behind the shop to make space for Dad's **SUPERHERO** games. They left the bin liners outside the shop because they thought some people might actually want some of it. When nothing was taken, Dad set up his **E-SELLALOT** account to sell it.

The other odd thing was what I could see sticking out of the bin liners. The leg of a broken action figurine. The sleeve of an old pair of Superman pyjamas that ꝶEAVEN had worn before me. Other items that were last seen taking up space in my wardrobe.

I decided to take the bin liners to the room at the back of the shop and open them up. Just to make sure.

**'AVENGERS ASSEMBLE!
WE HAVE A CUSTOMER!'**

That was the door, announcing my entry. It does that every time someone comes into our shop – a different one every day. ꝶEAVEN set up the system one day when he was bored.

I dragged the first bag in with a bit of help from Bilbo Baggins. You might know Bilbo Baggins as the hobbit from The Hobbit, but in our shop he's really Mr Shah from the retirement flats, who helps out while Dad's saving the world. Mr Shah likes dressing up as Bilbo, because the hairy feet keep his own feet warm.

I went out to fetch the second bin liner.

'BACK IN A FLASH.'

That was the door, announcing my exit. I managed to drag the second bin liner in by myself, as Mr Shah was busy trying on a **SPIDERMAN** mask.

As I suspected, both bin liners were full of my old stuff. I wasn't too bothered about throwing away my damaged and broken **SUPERHERO** figurines, and I hadn't worn many of the faded tee-shirts and pyjamas for a long time. But it was my stuff and I would have liked to throw it away myself.

Besides, I do have some things that I wouldn't want thrown away. Like any item of clothing that a normal girl might wear, that hasn't been worn by her brother before her. And *Mr Prickles*. I'd be very upset if *Mr Prickles* had been in that bin liner. He wasn't, but I ran upstairs into our flat above the shop, just to make sure he was all right.

As soon as I opened the door, I noticed a strange smell – sort of dusty and polishy at the same time. There were scrape marks on the thin strip of worn hall carpet you can see between all the boxes – like our old vacuum cleaner had been dragged over it.

Then something truly alarming happened.

'Hello, Tom!' Mum greeted me with a bright smile.

You might not think that was particularly alarming. But her smile was the one that looks as though it needs to be big enough to hide something. Then there was the high-pitched humming way she spoke, as though everything was just fine. But most worrying of all was the fact that Mum had her dangerous look on – the one where her eyes wander everywhere except where she wants to look. In this case, they were trying not to look upstairs.

Before I could ask her what was going on, she'd dashed into the living room and was sitting cross-legged on the floor going *ooooooohhhhhhhhmmmmmm!*

She does this to find her inner self. It's called yoga.

A GIRL called T.O.M.

It's best not to disturb Mum when she's trying to find her inner self. The last time I did, I discovered that her inner self is in fact a **BAD-TEMPERED DRAGON**.

I ran upstairs, but I opened the door to my room very slowly. I always do that, because you never know what's lurking in there. Like something that's escaped from one of ӇEAVEN'S experiments, or a robotic toy he's made that's triggered by movement and lights up with a lot of noise and waving of arms. Or an invisible laser beam that sets off an alarm when I step through it. But no. My room had none of that. It had something far more weird.

The smell of furniture polish nearly knocked me out. Everything on my chest of drawers had been squashed to one side, while the other side had polish smears all over it. Inside my wardrobe were three empty shelves smelling of furniture polish and three with my clothes crammed in. Half of the hanging rail had my clothes hanging from it and, underneath that, half a row of shoes.

I checked my chest of drawers. One drawer stuffed full. One empty and wafting furniture polish. Then I checked the windowsill, which is where **Mr Prickles** lives.

A GIRL called T.O.M.

He was still there. His pot was nice and clean, because that's how I like to keep it. The windowsill was clear of dust, because I like to keep it tidy for him. But now he was sharing the windowsill with Spidey-pig.

Spidey-pig is a piggy bank dressed as **SPIDERMAN**. Whenever you put money in him he says *thank you from your friendly neighbourhood Spiderman*. Even though he's a pig.

Spidey-pig hasn't thanked me very often, because Mum and Dad don't give me money – they say I can have whatever I want from the shop.

What was Mum thinking? She knows that Mr Prickles likes the windowsill all to himself. I put Spidey-pig back where he belonged.

In case you are wondering, Mr Prickles comes from Mexico and he is a Saguaro cactus. But he looks so much like a person that I call him **Mr Prickles**. Granny gave him to me after a trip to Mexico. She said she bought him from a botanical garden but, knowing Granny, she dug him up and smuggled him all the way to Pickford.

Mr Prickles is the only present Granny has brought back for me that I like.

'Well, **Mr Prickles**, do you have any idea what is going on?' I often talk to **Mr Prickles** – sometimes I think he's the only sensible member of my family. At least he never argues with me. And I often find the answer to my questions just by asking him. But this time I didn't. I'd have to ask Mum.

I went downstairs and sat cross-legged in front of her, until she'd finished her latest **Ohm**.

'Why have you cleared my room out?' I asked, before she could draw breath for the next one.

'Oh well, you know how it is.' She spoke in the sing-song voice with the dangerous smile. 'I'm teaching more yoga classes because the shop's not doing so well and Dad's going to need more time to start up his new line in **SUPERHERO** children's parties.'

I had heard them talking about the shop Being In Trouble and that they needed More Money to Keep it Going, but I didn't see what that had to do with the bin liners.

'As you know, Granny sold her flat before she went on her trip to Pemandagan, to buy a share in the business to help us out,' Mum said.

I didn't know.

'And that means,' continued Mum, 'we have to be extra nice to her, to thank her for helping us out.'

I made a note to try to like whatever Granny

brought back from Pemandagan.

'So…' continued Mum. 'Granny owns part of the flat as well. I told you all that this morning, didn't I?'

'This morning you asked me whether I wanted to share HEAVEN's room with him.'

'But I've decided you don't have to.' She smiled a smile that was volcano, earthquake, and end-of-the-world dangerous. 'You can share your room with Granny instead. I told you she'd have to live with us now, didn't I?'

'I don't think so,' I squeaked.

Chapter 4

Guess who came to collect us from school next day? Granny. She rushed into the playground, going as fast as she could with her legs wrapped up in a bright purple cloth, arms waving in a bright green shiny shirt.

'Thora, Thora, my darling Thora Odina!' She calls me that when she's not calling me her **Tom-Tom** girl.

She raced into the playground, arms wide open, while I watched from a safe distance behind a tree.

A GIRL called T.O.M.

'Where's my lovely **Tom-Tom** girl?' she asked Narinda, who shrugged and carried on talking to Elsa.

'She's hiding!' Lem pointed right at me.

I braced myself for Granny, who was now rushing towards me. But it's difficult to rush with your legs wrapped in a purple cloth, while trying to dodge a softball. Granny went splat. I ran straight over to see if she was all right.

A GIRL called T.O.M.

By the time I reached her, she was surrounded. She stayed on the ground, lifting her cloth all the way to her knickers, so everyone could see her grazed knees. '**Tom-Tom,** look what I've done!' she wailed up at me. 'I fell over!'

'Everyone can see what you've done,' I said. 'You can pull the cloth down now.'

'**IT'S NOT A CLOTH!**' she screeched. 'It's a longyi from Pemandagan. It's the height of fashion. The man who sold it to me said so.'

'Oh dear,' said a familiar voice. Mr Truber had come over to see what was going on. 'Mrs Fatbottom, are you all right?'

Granny's name really is Mrs Fatbottom. Mum was Miss Fatbottom until she married Dad and changed her name to Marvel. Mr Truber made me take Granny to Mrs Novak, the welfare assistant.

A GIRL called T.O.M.

'HELP, HELP!' cried Granny. 'SERIOUS INJURY! BLOOD! BLOOD!'

Mrs Novak came rushing out and saw me struggling along with Granny. 'Tom? What have you done to yourself?'

'IT'S NOT HER!' wailed Granny. 'IT'S ME!' She hobbled into Mrs Novak's office.

'Well,' said Mrs Novak. 'The thing is –' But she was interrupted by loud knocking on her open door. A girl from Reception was clutching her head and crying, while her mum looked worriedly at Mrs Novak.

'Oh dear,' said Mrs Novak. 'What happened, Grace?'

'I was here first!' Granny sat on the little chair.

'Er,' said Mrs Novak. 'That chair is for the kids to sit on?'

A GIRL called T.O.M.

'Look!' Granny lifted up her longyi and stuck her legs out. **'I'M BLEEDING!'**

Grace stopped crying and giggled. Mrs Novak sighed and found two big plasters for Granny, one for each knee. Granny hobbled out with a big grin on her face.

'You're funny,' said Grace.

Granny hobbled back to the playground, where the twins were being told off by Mr Truber. 'You know you are not allowed to kick footballs around the playground,' he said.

'It's a softball,' said Lem.

'Would you like to see my plasters?' Granny grabbed hold of the hem of her longyi.

'Granny!' I hissed. 'Mr Truber does not want to see your knees!' Or your knickers, I thought.

'Can I see?' Lem rushed over.

'Me first!' Kap tried to push him out of the way.

'Boys!' said Mr Truber. 'Tom's granny is wearing those plasters because of your carelessness. Now, stand still and say sorry to her.'

'Sorry,' said Kap. 'Cool plasters.'

'Sorry,' said Lem. 'Did you bring Tom some **POO?**'

'Would you like to come into class and tell us all about your trip to Pemandagan?' asked Mr Truber.

All the way home, Granny told us about her trip, loudly enough for the whole of Pickford to hear. She was staggering along with one arm around Lem and me and the other round Narinda and Kap. She didn't notice how people stopped and stared.

As soon as we arrived home, Granny's limp disappeared and she ran straight upstairs. 'You can help me unpack!' She made it sound like a big treat.

A GIRL called T.O.M.

The floor of my room was covered in suitcases, overflowing with longyis and bright shiny shirts.

'Ah, you like them!' said Granny. 'This one's for you!' She thrust the brightest shirt at me and, while I was trying not to be blinded by it, she rummaged around until she found the rest of my present – a bright pink longyi.

Then she ran to my brother, who was standing in the doorway. 'My HEAVENLY Boy!' Granny leapt into HEAVEN'S arms. I mean, she really did leap. HEAVEN is way taller than her and it's the only way she can plaster him with kisses.

'Hi Granny,' he said, once he'd managed to peel her off. 'I like your longyi.'

'I got one for you!' Granny shoved a bright yellow longyi at him. 'Tom called it a cloth!'

'Oh no,' said 𝒮HEAVEN. 'The longyi is the traditional dress of the Pemandagan Republic, formally known as Rubyland. And this is a lovely shirt. Thank you, Granny. Tom and I will wear these to school tomorrow.'

'What?'

Did I mention that my brother is the geekiest geek on planet Geek and I have no idea what he's doing on Earth? He has sticky-up hair, speaks Geek fluently, and I never know what he's talking about. I have long since learned to avoid saying *what?* Unfortunately, on this occasion I forgot.

A GIRL called T.O.M.

'I mean, what did you say about school?' I asked, before he could give me a lecture about longyis.

'I mean,' HEAVEN sighed, 'our parents are not in the habit of taking note of messages from school and neither are you. Just as well I like to keep myself informed. We both have non-uniform Friday tomorrow. I had prepared a suitable outfit for myself, but in honour of my grandmother's return, I'll be wearing my new longyi and shirt instead.'

'But you're in secondary school now,' I said. 'You don't dress up on non-uniform day.'

'Oh, Thora,' he sighed. 'If I turn up in normal clothes, there will be a lot of disappointed people at my school. They won't be able to tell me how cool I look.' In other words, everyone will laugh at him and ask him silly questions, so they can laugh even

A GIRL called T.O.M.

more while he tries to impart his knowledge while they're throwing things at him. I know all this from Narinda, whose brother is at HEAVEN'S school.

'And here's your extra special present!' Granny dug her hand into a suitcase and pulled out a fistful of gold chains. Not real gold – these looked like the ones that come from the Christmas crackers that haven't sold in Narinda's shop. They looked like they'd been made from paperclips. At the end of each chain was a red plastic jewel, the sort that go on the end of Christmas cracker chains.

'Giant rubies!'
Granny grinned.
'The man said
they will bring
us good luck for ever!'

A GIRL called T.O.M.

'If these really were giant rubies,' said HEAVEN, picking one up, 'you would have spent millions on them. Because rubies from Pemandagan are the most valuable in the world. And rubies this size are so rare you'd never find one, let alone this many.'

'But they look just like the real thing!' said Granny. 'The man said so.' She reached up and put a plastic ruby round HEAVEN's neck.

She put one round my neck as well. Despite being plastic, it was quite pretty.

You will not believe how much trouble those rubies would cause.

Chapter 5

That night I lay awake listening to the sounds coming up from my bottom bunk where Granny slept – *SNUFFLE, SNUFFLE, groomph, ghhhrrrr, SNORT, SNORT SNO– SNO– SNO– SNORE, SNOOOOOOORE!* Followed by a long, happy-sounding *Aaaaahhhh!* Then a very small pause, before it all started up again. Over and over until, suddenly, it went so quiet that I wondered if Granny had stopped breathing.

I thought I'd better check. I leaned over my top bunk, but heard nothing apart from my **STARSHIP ENTERPRISE** clock. I leaned over more, until my top half was all the way out and my hair was dangling nearly to the floor.

My hair brushed over Granny's face. Two gleaming eyes sprang open, her mouth widened, and out came a ***blood-curdling scream***. It gave me such a fright that I fell right out of my top bunk, ending in a heap on the floor.

The light went on and Mum burst in. 'What on earth is going on?'

'There was an evil face staring at me!' wailed Granny.

'I was worried about Granny,' I protested.

I thought Mum was going to tell Granny off for calling my face evil, but she turned her cross face to me instead. 'Honestly, Tom.' She tutted and gave me a warning look, which seemed to say *Be nice to Granny or we'll lose the shop.*

Then I had to have a talk about Being Silly and Waking Granny Up, from a man wearing **SPIDERMAN** pyjamas (aka my dad), before being told to go back to sleep. I think I did finally manage to sleep, because something woke me up.

Granny was moving about down there. 'I must be quiet,' she said in a loud whisper. 'I mustn't wake Tom up.' Thanks, Granny. 'But I really do need the toilet. Now, where's the door? I can't see in the dark. I will have to turn the light on.'

I cried out as the light pierced my eyes.

'Oh, you're awake anyway,' said Granny. 'I'm going to the toilet. I'll be back soon.'

She was ages. But eventually she shuffled in,

A GIRL called T.O.M.

fluffed up her duvet (loudly), got back into bed, got back out again, turned the light off, and fumbled her way (loudly) into bed.

Then the sound of Granny fast asleep started again . . .

'THE ENTERPRISE IS UNDER ATTACK! WAKE UP AND DO'

What?

'THE ENTERPRISE IS UNDER ATTACK!'

Oh no. I'd finally managed to fall asleep.

'WAKE UP AND DO SOMETHING!'

Only to be woken up by my Star Trek alarm clock.

'THE ENTERPRISE IS UNDER ATTACK!'

I fumbled about on my shelf to find it.

'WAKE UP AND DO SOMETHING!'

'I AM AWAKE AND I'M TRYING TO DO SOMETHING!'

Unfortunately, the something I did was knock it off my shelf.

A GIRL called T.O.M.

'What's going on?' Granny poked her head out from the bottom bunk. 'Why are you waking me up with all this –?' At exactly the wrong moment – **'AAARGGGGGHHH!'** – the Starship Enterprise landed on her head.

I came down to breakfast like a zombie who hasn't slept for a thousand years. Granny sat at the kitchen table, stirring her chocolate cereal, wearing a yellow longyi and a bright orange shirt, her plastic ruby on a chain and two plasters on her head, forming an 'X' where the Enterprise had landed.

I picked up the packet of chocolate cereal. It was empty. I didn't bother looking in the cupboard for another one. Mum always waits until we run out of things and then goes next door.

A GIRL called T.O.M.

'Ah, just the right shade of chocolatey brown,' said Granny.

'Has Mum gone next door for more?' I asked.

'No, she's gone to buy more plasters, as she used the last one on my head.'

I decided I'd have muesli.

'You shouldn't eat that,' said Granny, through a mouthful of chocolate cereal. 'It's full of sugar.'

'Quite right,' said HEAVEN, coming in wearing his longyi and shiny shirt, plastic ruby dangling. 'Granny, whatever happened to your head?'

'Tom dropped her alarm clock on it,' said Mum, coming in wearing her longyi, shirt, and ruby.

'You should be more careful,' said Dad, coming in wearing – well, you can guess.

I sat surrounded by people looking like extras from a movie called **THE CLASH OF THE COLOURS**.

A GIRL called T.O.M.

'Why aren't you wearing your longyi?' asked Dad, giving my nice jeans and tee-shirt a look of disgust.

A GIRL called T.O.M.

'Because Tom does not wish to be distinguished from the ordinary,' said HEAVEN.

'I want to be ordinary,' I said. 'Ordinary's good.'

'Ordinary is for people to hide behind, for fear of being who they really are,' said HEAVEN.

'I know who I really am,' I said. 'I'm an ordinary, normal girl, wearing ordinary, normal clothes.'

'Don't you want to wear what I brought you all the way back from Pemandagan?' asked Granny, stroking the plaster on her forehead. 'Don't you like it?'

'Of course she likes it,' said Dad. 'She doesn't want to spoil it by getting chocolate cereal down it. Or muesli.' He gave me the Be Nice to Granny warning look.

I had no choice but to change. 'The things I do to keep our shop,' I muttered to Mr Prickles, as I tied the longyi round my waist.

A GIRL called T.O.M.

At school I was so tired that I hardly noticed everyone asking me why I was wearing a tablecloth. I hardly noticed that Narinda and Elsa were wearing the same jeans and top. I was so tired that Mr Truber had to wake me up twice. The third time, I woke up with a scream.

'Having a bad dream, Tom?' asked Mr Truber, while the rest of the class laughed. But he was right – I was dreaming that Granny was sharing my room, only to wake up and find it was true. Then Mr Truber asked me to stand in front of the class and tell everyone about what I was wearing.

'It's from Pemandagan,' I said. 'It's called a longyi and the shirt is the height of fashion. That's what my granny said, anyway.'

'I think you are very lucky,' said Mr Truber. 'To

have a granny to bring you all these wonderful gifts from exotic places.'

That's not quite how I'd have put it.

'Let's see what else we can find out about Pemandagan.' Mr Truber brought a website up on the screen. 'It used to be called Rubyland and is the world's largest producer of rubies. So, that's why you're wearing a ruby round your neck.'

I wish he hadn't said that. Some of the kids thought it was a real ruby and thought it would be fun to chase me round the playground for it. It's difficult to run in a longyi, but luckily I didn't fall over like Granny did.

Chapter 6

Granny was too busy to come and collect us from school, so we walked home with Fifi, the twins' mum. Fifi is a tall fluffy lady with freckles and waves of fair hair. She has big blue eyes, never stops smiling, and talks like she's singing a lullaby. She wears long flowing dresses and thinks everything is wonderful, especially her twins.

Mr Truber doesn't agree. 'Your boys have been fighting again, Ms Lavender.'

'Oh, poor Mr Truber!' she sings. 'Your karma is

very negative. Why don't you pop by my shop and I'll see what I can do for you?'

In case you're wondering, karma is something everyone is born with. It can be negative or positive. The more negative it is, the more things you can buy in Fifi's shop to help.

Fifi's karma lets her wander into the road with a big smile, because her karma is powerful enough to stop a bus. It is certainly enough to cause a lot of beeping and screeching of tyres.

Luckily, the rest of us have karma that makes us wait for the green man before crossing.

The twins have karma that makes them fight all the time. Fifi lets them – if they hurt themselves it's down to their karma. This time they were so bad that they crashed into me and sent me banging into a man who was innocently walking along.

A GIRL called T.O.M.

'You stupid girl!' the man snarled. He was probably glaring as well, but I couldn't tell as his eyes were hidden behind dark glasses.

'But it wasn't –'

'She's very sorry,' said Lem, pulling me away.

'Yes, she is,' said Kap, grabbing my other arm.

'But it was you!' I struggled.

'Shh!' hissed Kap. 'We don't want him to know we were on to him.'

'What are you talking about?'

'He's been following us all the way from school. We pushed you into him deliberately.'

'You pushed me into him because you were fighting,' I said.

'We were only pretending to fight,' said Lem.

I laughed. 'Are you always pretending then? Because that looked pretty real to me.'

A GIRL called T.O.M.

'We were fighting for real to start with,' said Kap. 'Then we noticed that man following us. Don't look behind you, but he's still acting suspiciously.'

I sneaked a look. The man was picking something up from the ground. He must have dropped it when the boys made me bang into him. They ran off ahead, laughing and fighting all the way home. While Fifi floated into her shop, they ran round the back to let themselves into their flat.

A GIRL called T.O.M.

Fifi's shop is called *Fifi's*. It sells candles, crystals, stones, and other items to bring you inner peace. Today it had a notice in the window.

> ## New in!
> ### Precious ruby stones
> ### to heal your heart
> ### and mind

The precious ruby stones looked a lot like the one that was hanging round my neck.

Only it wasn't. The chain must have snapped and fallen off – probably when I'd bumped into the man with the dark glasses. That must have been what he was picking up! He wasn't being suspicious at all – he was probably wondering who'd dropped it.

Our shop also had a notice.

> # New in!
> ## The red Power Gem
> ## – access to great power
> ## to all who possess it!
> ## Hurry while stocks last!

You can guess what the red *Power Gems* were. Then, as Narinda went next door, I saw a notice in their window.

Their shop is called **PICKFORD NEWS AND GENERAL STORE.** It's a shop where you can buy almost anything and I love going in there to see what I can find. Narinda's mum, Mrs Singh, often lets me have items that have reached the end of the line – like the tee-shirt I was wearing this morning before I had to change.

There are always notices in the window, about special offers and things. And today there was a new one.

> # New in!
>
> *Lovely ruby pendants –*
> *a perfect gift for a special*
> *person!*

Granny must have bought a lot of plastic rubies. The door announced my arrival.

**'ODIN'S BEARD
IT'S A CUSTOMER!'**

Dad looked up as I came in. He was behind the counter, in his longyi and shiny shirt, wearing a long blond wig and false beard – in other words, he was Thor after a trip to Pemandagan.

'Ah good, you're back,' he said. He often says this – it means he has a job for me. 'Granny needs your help. She's trying to set up an account on **E-SELLALOT** to sell these longyis.' He pointed to the pile of longyis on the counter, with a note on top that said *Superhero capes in all colours – buy two get one free!*

I know how to use **E-SELLALOT** because I help Dad with it. All you do is think of a username and a password, and you have an account. Then you have to take photos of what you want to sell and think up interesting descriptions.

'ODIN'S BEARD IT'S A CUSTOMER!'

A GIRL called T.O.M.

It was the man the twins had made me bump into. He must have followed me here and now he'd come to give me my ruby back. But he walked right past me, up to the counter, and stared at Dad, the light glinting on his dark glasses. He didn't look like our normal sort of customer.

'Give me all your red power gems.' He pointed to the small basket of plastic rubies, with a note that said *Buy your red Power Gem – while stocks last!* He was wearing a black suit and white shirt. He looked very neat and very still.

'I wouldn't advise it,' said Dad. 'You could do a lot of damage with all that power.'

'Just give me your power gems.' He was no bigger than my dad and spoke quietly, but he sounded powerful enough not to need any power gems.

'Of course,' said Dad, tipping the basket of plastic

rubies into a bag. 'They're £2.50 each, so that'll be £50 altogether, please.'

'And the one round your neck,' said the customer. Dad took the ruby from round his neck and handed it over. 'That'll be £2.50 extra, for the chain.'

'And the one in the window,' said the man.

'Of course. Tom?' Dad tipped his head towards the window.

I fetched the ruby. When I came back, the customer was still standing like a statue while Dad was making his **Be Friendly to all Customers** smiley face at him. 'I'll pop a leaflet in the bag. It's all about our special offers and our new line in children's parties.'

I didn't think he looked much like someone who'd be interested in children's parties. He stuffed the bag into his pocket. It was nearly all the way in, when I noticed a small piece of gold chain peeking from his pocket. One that looked like it had been made from paperclips. The chain that held my ruby!

'Don't forget,' Dad called after him as he walked

out of the shop without a word. 'With great power comes great responsibility!' said the door.

'HAH, HAH,
YOU'LL BE BACK,'

I hoped he wasn't back. There was something very creepy about him. So creepy that I didn't say anything about the fact that he stole my ruby. Although I had no idea why he'd want a load of plastic rubies.

'That's the best sale I've made all day,' said Dad.

'ODIN'S BEARD
IT'S A CUSTOMER!'

For a horrible moment, I thought the customer

had come back. But it was the twins. 'Mum asked us to come and fight in here instead of upstairs in the flat!' said Lem.

'Because she can hear us thumping around up there!' said Kap, picking up a lightsaber.

'Where's Serafina?' asked Dad. Serafina is the lady who helps out in Fifi's shop and stays in the flat with the twins sometimes. Fifi employed her because she has good karma and dark, mysterious eyes.

'She's busy polishing rubies.' Lem picked up a replica of **THOR'S** hammer. He swung it at Kap, who ducked, took a swing at Lem with his lightsaber, but missed. Dad tutted. Lem tried again. This time he scored a hit.

'Aargh!' Kap clutched his head. 'Mr Marvel, he's killed me!'

'Of course he has,' said Dad. 'If you want to beat

A GIRL called T.O.M.

THOR'S hammer with a lightsaber, this is how you do it.' He came out from the counter, and before Kap knew it, flicked the lightsaber from his hand. Then, before Lem knew it, he flipped **THOR'S** hammer out of his hand with it.

'Hey!' protested Kap, trying to snatch it back.

But Dad was too quick. 'If you're going to fight in my shop,' he said, 'at least learn to do it properly.'

I left him to give the boys a lesson in lightsaber versus hammer fighting. I'd gone as far as the bottom of the stairs when I heard a crash. Followed by a yelp. From Dad. I think the boys were learning fast.

I found Granny in the living room hunched over the table, surrounded by bin liners, having an argument with the computer. 'Why can't I have *Tom* as my password? Who says it hasn't got enough letters? Ah, Tom, good, come and tell this computer it's being stupid and to let me put my stuff on **E-SELLALOT**.'

'You need to think of a username,' I said.

'Granny Fatbottom's Emporium of Delights,' said Granny.

'It needs to be shorter than that, and one word.'

'Why?'

This was going to take a long time.

Chapter 7

Eventually, with a lot of arguing from Granny, we set up her **E-SELLALOT** account. Username **THORASGRANNYISGR8**, password unknown, as Granny made me look away while she typed it in. I had to look away a lot – it took a long time to find a password that satisfied both **E-SELLALOT** and Granny.

'Now, we can start selling.' She tipped one of the bin liners over and spilled its contents everywhere. 'You can sell anything on **E-SELLALOT**,' she grinned.

A GIRL called T.O.M.

Granny took hundreds of photos and made me put in the descriptions. 'Describe the pyjamas as new and unworn!' she demanded. 'Then we'll get more money and I can go on another trip.'

It would take a mountain of pyjamas to pay for another trip. 'But these have been worn by both HEAVEN and me,' I said. 'If you sell these as new, that's fraud.'

'What's fraud?' HEAVEN came in, back from school in his longyi and shirt and a face that looked like it had just met a lamppost. His nose was swollen and one of his eyes was nearly closed.

'Oh, my poor HEAVENLY Boy!' Granny rushed to him. 'What happened?'

Unfortunately, I could guess. 'Was it the kids at school?' I asked. 'I told you not to wear those clothes.'

'On the contrary,' said ƎHEAVEN. 'At school everyone was most interested by my outfit and replica priceless ruby.' He tapped his chest, but there was no ruby there. 'Unfortunately, I was divested of my ruby on the way home. I was walking along, thinking about **Einstein's theory of relativity,** when someone in an awful hurry ran past me. A gentleman in a smart suit. As he sped by, his fingers caught the chain of my ruby and it snapped clean off. Despite calling after the gentleman, he didn't hear me and disappeared into the crowd.'

'What crowd?' I asked.

'The one that gathered when I bumped into a lamppost I hadn't noticed while I was running after the gentleman. But he carried on with the chain dangling from his hand. Probably didn't see what he'd done because he was wearing dark glasses.'

Dark glasses? Smart suit? I knew exactly who it was. But why?

'Never mind,' said Granny. 'There are plenty more rubies for sale next door. Tom, go and get one while I attend to ꙮHEAVEN.' Then she screwed her face up at me. 'Where's your ruby?'

'I lost it the same way as ꙮHEAVEN,' I said. 'But without the lamppost.'

I could tell neither of them believed me. 'Get two then,' said Granny.

I went down through the shop, where I found Dad sitting on the floor, surrounded by fallen displays of comic books, action figurines, **SUPERHERO** DVDs, and most of the contents of the shop's first aid box. Standing behind him, holding Dad's head back while he clutched a wad of cotton wool under his nose, was Mr Truber.

I probably haven't mentioned this, but Mr Truber is one of Dad's best customers.

'Those boys are uncontrollable,' said Mr Truber. 'I hope they haven't broken your nose.'

'No, no,' said Dad. It sounded more like *doe, doe*. 'Dey were just learning how to fight. I ducked at the wrong time and my nose met a lightsaber.'

'From what I've seen at school, those boys already know perfectly well how to fight.'

A GIRL called T.O.M.

That was me, leaving the shop. I went next door to **PICKFORD NEWS AND GENERAL STORE**, where I found Narinda's mum behind the counter.

'Can I help you?' she smiled.

'I need two of Granny's ruby pendants,' I said.

'Oh dear, I'm afraid I can't help you with that,' she said. 'A man came in and bought them all. Strange customer, didn't say much, and he wore dark glasses, so I couldn't see him properly. Smart suit, though. I don't think he's from around here. Why don't you try Fifi's? She was selling some as well.'

I arrived at Fifi's in time to see Serafina taking down the sign offering healing rubies for sale. She was holding an empty basket. I didn't need to go in to ask her who'd bought them all.

Back in the shop, Mr Truber was tidying up, while Dad was behind the counter, wearing a Wookiee hood. 'Don't want to frighten the customers with my swollen nose,' he said.

I went back upstairs to have a little chat with **Mr Prickles**. 'Who would want to buy all of Granny's rubies?' I asked him. 'How am I going to tell Granny that I can't replace the one I lost? Maybe I could tell her they've all been sold, so she can start saving for her next trip – she'll be too pleased to worry about the one I lost.'

Like I said, **Mr Prickles** always helps me to find an answer.

I went downstairs to tell Granny the good news. But she came out of the kitchen, wielding a small axe.

'Hah, there you are!' she said, eyes glinting. That's when I noticed she was wearing an apron – and it had bloodstains on it.

A GIRL called T.O.M.

That's when I realised that the axe wasn't a prop from the shop. It was real.

'That's a very nice axe,' I said, trying to keep calm.

'Axe?' she laughed. 'This is a cleaver – for chopping food. The man I bought it from said it's sharp enough to chop off your fingers. I'm using it to prepare dinner. Come and help me!'

I followed her into the kitchen. Axe or cleaver, I wasn't going to argue.

Chapter 8

You will not believe what Granny had done to our kitchen. Here is a list, in no particular order:

- (If you are a vegetarian, look away now.)
- The table was covered with heaps of chopped raw meat, with blood dribbling everywhere.
- Several open recipe books lay about, their pages marked with bloody fingerprints.
- (OK vegetarians, you can look now.)
- There were dangerous-looking knives everywhere.

- There was raw vegetable matter everywhere.
- There was raw meat everywhere (oops – sorry, vegetarians!)
- There was a mad axe/cleaver-wielding granny blocking my exit.

A GIRL called T.O.M.

'I'm making chop suey!' said Granny. She raised her cleaver and brought it crashing down on some poor vegetable, shattering it into pieces that went everywhere. 'So start chopping!'

More like bomb suey, I thought, but decided it was best not to say anything. I picked up the safest-looking knife and chopped until my arms ached.

Granny picked up a wok. 'All we have to do is put it in here and cook it!'

I looked at the size of the wok and the pile of chopped food. 'It won't fit.'

'Of course it will, if we do a bit at a time.'

Granny then showed me how to cook chop suey – by setting fire to the wok. The alarm went off and the sprinkler system came on. Granny thought it was hilarious – especially as I was the one who got soaked.

Somehow I managed to stay alive until it was all cooked. Then all I could do was slump at the table.

'This is delicious,' I heard Mum say from the other side of the mound of food. 'Thanks for cooking.'

'I'll do the cooking now!' said Granny. 'We'll eat healthy food like this all the time!'

Despite being too exhausted to eat, I have to admit it didn't taste too bad. But I wish I'd known the trouble Granny's cooking was going to cause.

'ENTERPRISE HLVLU'
YLLEM 'EJ VAY YLTA.'

What?

'ENTERPRISE HLVLU'
YLLEM 'EJ VAY YLTA.'

My alarm clock was set to Klingon.

'ENTERPRISE HLVLU' YLLEM 'EJ VAY YLTA.'

My alarm was going off, despite it being Saturday. ℋEAVEN must have been in and reset it. He does that sometimes, for a laugh.

'NuqneH.'

What? It sounded like the Klingon greeting, coming from my bottom bunk, but in a strange, muffled voice.

I stuck my head over. '**AARGH!!**' I screamed. Granny's face was all pinched and puffy and shining with sweat. One eye was missing and it looked like the rest of her face was being eaten by a mad sea monster with waving tentacles. Then I realised that she was wearing a Borg mask.

A GIRL called T.O.M.

[In case you don't know, the Borg are from Star Trek. They are part human, part machine, and all evil. And very ugly.]

'Why are you wearing a Borg mask?' I asked.

'To protect me from your alarm clock.' Granny took the mask off, making her hair stick up everywhere. 'Heh, heh.' That's not Klingon – it's the way Granny laughs. 'We set the alarm to Klingon.'

'But it's Saturday,' I said, flicking the switch to turn it off.

A GIRL called T.O.M.

The alarm clock went bonkers. A siren screeched and a voice warned of my imminent grizzly death for tampering with it. At the same time, Granny doubled over laughing. **'WE TRICKED YOU!'** she screeched. **'HEH, HEH, HEH!'**

It didn't matter what I did, I couldn't shut it up. Until a grinning ℋEAVEN came in, looking like he was wearing a Borg mask, but it was just his own face with black eye and swollen nose from hitting that lamppost. He high-fived Granny, took the alarm clock, fiddled with it for a split second, and shut it up.

I decided I'd go to Narinda's and stay there all day. And the next day. And every day for ever.

'I'm off next door,' I said, standing at the kitchen doorway. Granny and ℋEAVEN were sitting at the table eating leftover chop suey and discussing the theory of evolution.

'Don't worry,' said Granny. 'One day humans will evolve with tough faces, so it doesn't matter if they bump into lampposts.'

'Or they'll invent councils who don't put up solid lampposts in silly places,' said HEAVEN.

'Anyway, bye,' I said.

'Where are you going?' demanded Granny.

'Next door.'

'Oh good,' she said. 'You can help me carry.'

Granny and I arrived in **PICKFORD NEWS AND GENERAL STORES** with our arms piled high with longyis. I had to stand there while my arms ached and Granny had a discussion with Narinda's dad about selling longyis, while peeping over the top of her pile.

A GIRL called T.O.M.

'I know we sold the rubies very quickly,' said Mr Singh. 'But –'

'The man who sold these longyis to me said they were perfect for selling in your shop.' Granny dumped her load on top of the newspaper on the counter. The one a customer had just put there to pay for it.

'Would you like a longyi?' Granny asked him. 'All the way from Pemandagan.'

'No thanks,' said the customer, trying to move his paper out and ripping it.

'Never mind,' said Mr Singh. 'Take another paper. You can have it for free.'

'Thank you,' said the customer. He was just about to go, when he stopped and stared at Granny. Then he shook himself and left.

People often stare at Granny – I'm quite used to

it. But this man wasn't looking her up and down in wonder like most people do when they try to work out what she's wearing (in this case she was still dressed like a fashion disaster from Pemandagan). This man was staring right at her ruby – as though it really was a power gem.

As he left, I noticed that he was wearing a longyi.

Chapter 9

I like it at Narinda's. It's quiet and peaceful and you can go from room to room without bumping into boxes or falling over someone doing yoga. Her older brother never stops to lecture you about how long the world is going to last or why cows eat green grass and produce white milk.

Narinda sat at her desk, listening to music through one earphone, while I sat on her bed with the other earphone in my ear.

'You're so lucky,' I said. 'I wish I could live

somewhere peaceful like this.' That was the last thing I remember.

'Tom?' Someone was gently shaking me. 'Wake up and –'

I sat up. 'Do something!' I shouted, desperately reaching for my alarm clock. It wasn't there. Just Narinda's mum peering at me.

'Your granny says you have to go home now,' she said. 'To eat some lovely lunch. And your mum would like you to bring some milk.'

I went through their shop to collect the milk. Narinda's dad was trying to display a heap of longyis.

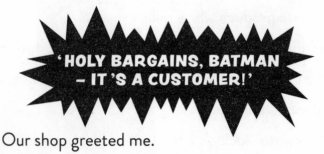

'HOLY BARGAINS, BATMAN – IT'S A CUSTOMER!'

Our shop greeted me.

A GIRL called T.O.M.

Dad was dressed as **BATMAN** and talking to a customer I recognised. It was the man in the longyi, who'd been staring at Granny's ruby.

'Will that be all?' said Dad, putting a false beard and moustache into a paper bag.

'I'd like to wear them now,' said the customer. He ripped open the packet, peeled off the protective tape and stuck his new beard and moustache on. 'How do I look?'

'Can I help you?' said Dad, like the man was a new customer.

'I heard you had *red power gems* for sale,' said the customer, in a different voice.

'I've sold out of the red ones,' said Dad. 'But I do have space gems, time gems, soul gems, mind gems, and reality gems. Then I've got –'

'No thank you,' said the customer. He turned and left, but I'm sure he frowned at me before he did.

'Try **E-SELLALOT**!' Dad called after him.

'FAREWELL, MY FRIENDS,'

said the door.

'Farewell,' said the customer.

'Why do you think he wanted one of Granny's

plastic – I mean **red power gems**?' I asked Dad.

'Perhaps he has them all apart from that one,' said Dad. 'He will be a very powerful man if finds it.'

I shouldn't have expected a sensible answer. I went up to the flat.

'Come and have some chop suey!' Granny steered me into the kitchen, where the pile of chop suey didn't look any smaller.

'Oh,' said HEAVEN. 'I see you fell asleep while listening to music at Narinda's.'

'How do you know?' I asked. 'You haven't been using your remote-controlled mobile mini webcam, have you? You know it's illegal to spy.'

'I am aware of that,' he said. 'I can tell, because you have a red line down your cheek that matches the wire from a set of earphones. This signifies that your cheek spent a lot of time in heavy contact with it. As it was your left cheek against it, that means your left brain was resting, which is the best side for sleep.'

I lifted my hand and felt the dent down my face. That was why Narinda's mum laughed when I woke up. Maybe that's why the customer in the longyi frowned at me before he left the shop.

YOU – SHALL – NOT – PASS!!

I'd finally fallen asleep when the stern voice of Gandalf the wizard roared around the flat. [In case you don't know, Gandalf is the wizard from The Hobbit. Mostly he's friendly, but he can be bad-tempered and fierce. Especially if you are a baddy.]

YOU – SHALL – NOT – PASS!!

A GIRL called T.O.M.

I'd only ever heard Gandalf in the flat once before – when **HEAVEN** was testing out his intruder alarm. He said it would be more effective than a normal alarm. And just to make sure, he connected it to the local police station.

YOU – SHALL – NOT – PASS!!

We had an intruder!

YOU – SHALL – NOT – PASS!!

I curled up into a ball and put my pillow over my head.

Then a thump, a scream, gunshots, machine gun fire, and several explosions. Followed by wailing sirens so loud it felt like they were whizzing around in my head. Then the light went on.

I sat up. I screamed. Then I realised it was only Dad in his **HULK** costume, with his evil clown mask on top.

He took the mask off. 'You can turn it off now, ♀HEAVEN!' he shouted. The screams, sirens, gunfire, and explosions stopped. 'It's all right, Tom, it's all safe now. We had an intruder, but he took one look at me and ran off.'

Mum came running in. 'Tom, are you all right? Mum?' She peered into the bottom bunk. 'Mum?' Granny answered with a snore. 'I can't believe she's still sleeping. The police will be here soon. I'll go and put the kettle on.' She always does this when there's a crisis. I have never understood why. 'Leave the light on, Jim.'

A GIRL called T.O.M.

They went out, leaving the light on and the door open. I climbed down from my bunk and went to the window. 'It's all right,' I told **Mr Prickles**, but my voice was a bit shaky. 'He's gone. You're safe.'

'Why did you put the light on?' Granny's shrill voice made me jump.

'We had an intruder,' I explained. 'Look, the police have come.' I could see blue flashing lights outside our shop down below. The police were talking to the **HULK**, aka Dad, while trying to calm down a hysterical woman in a fluffy pink dressing gown, aka Fifi. Then they were joined by a normal-looking man and woman, aka Narinda's parents.

'I'll warm up the wok,' said Granny.

Eventually, the police assured Fifi that they would

deal with their karma and that her boys were safe from the intruder, although they wouldn't like to say whether the intruder would be safe from them. They praised **HEAVEN** for his alarm. By that time they were in our kitchen, the kettle had boiled, the wok had warmed, and the police were sitting round our table, drinking tea and eating chop suey. By police, I mean Sergeant Ben and her deputy, PC Meer. They are both customers of Dad's.

'It looks like three shops downstairs were broken into,' said Sergeant Ben. 'Fifi's, **PICKFORD NEWS**, and **SUPERHERO**. But yours is the only flat the intruder came into. He seems to have got away empty-handed.'

'Thanks to your alarm system,' said PC Meer, leaning back and patting his chop suey-filled stomach.

A GIRL called T.O.M.

'Thank you,' said HEAVEN. Then he gave them a lecture on how he'd wired it, by the end of which I was fast asleep.

Chapter 10

On Sunday morning, Dad sent me to Fifi's to see if she was all right after last night's break-in.

Welcome! said her door, in a soothing voice. Her shop was filled with dangly chime music, which Fifi plays to ward off evil spirits. She also burns candles, the smell of which is enough to put off the good spirits as well.

Fifi was deep in conversation with Narinda's dad and didn't hear me coming in. 'It was those rubies, Mr Singh,' she was saying. 'Terrible karma. I should never have agreed to sell them in my shop. I tried to warn the man who bought them.'

'But they were only plastic,' said Mr Singh.

'Exactly!' wailed Fifi. 'Think of the negative karma from a single false gem, let alone all of them. I was very glad to tell the man who came in yesterday that there were none left.'

'The man with the false beard?' said Mr Singh. 'He came into our shop as well. Seemed devastated that we had no plastic ruby pendants left. Oh, hello, Tom. I hope you aren't still after a ruby?'

I told them I was fine. But I couldn't help wondering what was going on with men in dark glasses and men in false beards who suddenly wanted to buy plastic rubies.

As I left Fifi's, I saw Narinda waiting outside her shop. 'Guess what?' I said. 'Someone's been –'

'I know,' she said. 'Mum and Dad told me about it this morning. I didn't hear a thing, so I didn't know about the break-ins until this morning. Apparently ℋEAVEN'S alarm sent the intruder running.'

'Yes, but –'

'Anyway, Elsa should be here soon.'

'Elsa?'

'Her mum's picking me up and we're going shopping.'

'Oh.' I suddenly began to feel a bit cold. 'I wish I could come shopping with you.'

'We didn't ask you, because you never have any money.'

That was true. Whenever I asked for money, I was told I could go down to our shop and have whatever I liked.

'You could ask your dad for some money,' said Narinda. 'I'll wait for you.'

A GIRL called T.O.M.

I ran into our shop.

'BY THE HAIRY HOSTS OF HOGARTH,'

'IT'S A CUSTOMER.'

said the door.

Dad was dressed as Dr Strange, to go with the announcement. Mr T (aka Mr Truber) was helping in the shop. That meant he was leaning on the counter talking to Dad about the intruder.

'Funny how nothing was stolen,' said Mr T.

Did I mention that Mr Truber sometimes comes to the shop dressed as Mr T? [In case you don't know, Mr T is the name of the actor who played a character called B.A. in an older version of The A-Team. Mr T is a huge, muscly guy with a Mohawk hairstyle and lots of gold chains around his neck.

He often wears combats and always looks like someone you don't want to mess with.]

Mr Truber wore a piece of moulded black foam on his bald head, purchased from our shop some time ago, so it now has a few dents in it. He had a false beard and moustache that were looking a bit worn. Round his neck hung a bunch of gold chains bought from our shop. His combats were baggy on him, because he is a lot thinner than the real Mr T.

To be honest, he looks nothing like Mr T.

'They didn't steal anything from next door either,' said Dad. 'Nor anything from Fifi's.'

'The boys probably scared him off,' said Mr T.

'Dad?' I said. He ignored me. 'Sorry, Dr Strange. Could I have some money?'

'Whatever for?'

'I want to go shopping with Narinda and Elsa. I

need it right now.'

'You can't go shopping,' he said. 'Granny needs you upstairs.' He went back to talking to Mr Truber.

I went up to the flat. The kitchen door was open and there were very strange noises coming from it. I think Granny was trying to teach ꪖHEAVEN to speak Pemandagan, while ꪖHEAVEN was trying to teach Granny the periodic table which, as far as I know, has something to do with science. I crept past and went up to my room.

I had an urgent meeting with Spidey-pig.

Spidey-pig was still on my chest of drawers, squashed along with everything Mum had pushed over to make room for Granny. Her side was littered with brushes, combs, hair clips, perfume, old make-up, a bulging handbag, and several scrunched-up shopping receipts.

I picked Spidey-pig up. If only I could open him.

You wouldn't think it would be difficult to open a Spiderman piggy bank. But when you have a brother like mine, even the simplest things become impossible. I'd have to take Spidey-pig downstairs to ask HEAVEN how to work the foolproof lock he'd put on there.

I'd just picked Spidey-pig up when I heard Narinda's voice calling me. I went to the window, to see that a car had squeezed in behind the Batmobile. Narinda looked up towards my window and shouted something. I couldn't quite hear what it was, but I heard Granny calling from the kitchen window below. 'She can't come shopping! She's helping me all afternoon and anyway, she has no money!'

A GIRL called T.O.M.

I watched Narinda turn away and climb into the car. As it drove off, I caught a glimpse of the back of her head as she turned towards Elsa.

That was when I noticed that Mr Prickles was missing.

I ran downstairs.

'Ah, good, Tom!' Granny came out of the kitchen. 'You can help me –'

'What have you done with Mr Prickles?' I shouted.

'Who?'

'Mr Prickles,' explained HEAVEN, 'is the name Tom gave to her Saguaro cactus. Which is not a very accurate name, because –'

I didn't hear the rest. I'd seen my poor Mr Prickles, sitting on the draining board, looking very sorry for himself.

'I gave him a wash!' said Granny, beaming.

A GIRL called T.O.M.

A wash? His pot was flooded with water and his prickles were dripping. Everyone knows that cacti come from deserts and need very little water. I do give **Mr Prickles** water from time to time, but I know how important it is not to give him too much – because he'll die.

'You've drowned him!' I picked up the pot, to show Granny the water swimming around at the top of his pot.

A GIRL called T.O.M.

Granny grabbed the pot from me. 'Don't be silly – we can empty the water out.' She tipped the pot over the sink, where bits of washing-up stuck out from a thick layer of soap bubbles. I could do nothing but watch helplessly as soil, cactus, and all fell from the pot and disappeared under the foam.

'Now look what you've made me do,' accused Granny, making a grab for poor **Mr Prickles**. 'Ouch!' She drew her hand back as he prickled her. 'Ouch!' she said, as she went in with the other hand.

Then she went in with both hands and dragged poor **Mr Prickles** out by his roots. There was no soil left now. 'That cactus has ruined my washing-up!' she complained, dumping him on the draining board. 'I'll have to empty all the water out and start again.' She stuck her hand in to find the plug. 'Ouch!' She brought her hand out. Instead of the plug, one of **Mr Prickles**'s arms was squeezed between her finger and thumb.

'What is going on?' Mum stumbled in, looking like she'd just woken up from a deep sleep. 'I'm trying to meditate.'

'Look what Granny's done!' I pointed to where poor **Mr Prickles** lay on the draining board, all soggy with his roots completely naked and an arm missing. Granny couldn't speak, because she was trying to suck prickles out of her fingers.

'Oh dear,' said Mum. 'Tom, go and fetch some plasters for your poor granny.'

What?

Chapter 11

I refused to help Granny with **E-SELLALOT** until **Mr Prickles** was back on my windowsill. He had a very clean pot and some new soil from the hardware store next to **PICKFORD NEWS**. Next to him was a smaller pot, where **HEAVEN** had insisted I plant **Mr Prickles**'s arm.

According to my brother, a cactus can regenerate from a single limb.

I went downstairs. **HEAVEN** and Granny were still in the kitchen, having a conversation in

A GIRL called T.O.M.

Pemandagan, as though nothing had happened.
I went into the living room. Mum was lying on
the floor on her back, fast asleep – she calls this
meditation, or being at peace with her inner self.

I slumped on the swivel chair by the table, which
gave a little swing, so I ended up facing the computer.
I looked at the screen.

E-SELLALOT!
Where you can sell anything online!

Anything?

Have an unwanted item causing you stress?

Did I have an unwanted item causing me stress?
I thought about how I should have been shopping
with Narinda and Elsa, while Mr Prickles was safely

in one piece on my windowsill, in my own room. I certainly did have something very unwanted – and she was causing me a lot of stress.

Click here to open an account and start selling!

I looked at Mum, lying on the floor. She was obviously very much at peace with her inner self. I heard laughter from the kitchen. I clicked *here*.

Choose a username.

I chose a username. NormalGirl.

Choose a password.

I chose a password. IamSoNormal!!! I typed it in again, as requested.

Just take a photo and start selling!

A GIRL called T.O.M.

I took the camera to the kitchen. Granny was now shrieking at 𝓗EAVEN in Pemandagan, waving a large cucumber in one hand and her cleaver in the other. She still had a plaster on her head as well as one on every single finger and her apron had bloodstains on it. She didn't notice me taking her picture.

I uploaded the photo. I filled in all the required fields.

Click <u>continue</u> to see what your ad will look like on our site!

I clicked.

Lot No 8730652998 (antiques)

– One Granny for sale!

A GIRL called T.O.M.

Condition: Old and loud

Postage options: Too heavy to post. Will object to being wrapped up and sent by courier. Better to collect in person. Or make arrangements for public transport. She's good at getting buses and trains. And planes.

Returns policy: ABSOLUTELY NO RETURNS!!

A GIRL called T.O.M.

Description of Lot:

One Granny, old but good condition. Loves travelling, cooking 'healthy' food, and being 'helpful'. Currently sleeping in granddaughter's bedroom and would like to move out.

SOLD WITHOUT RESERVE—PLEASE BID!

Bidding ends on Saturday at 3pm.

Click continue to list your item and wait for the bids to come in!

So there I was. One click away.

But then I thought about how much trouble I'd be in if anyone found out I'd tried to sell my own grandmother, even though I had good reason to.

A **thumping** and **THUDDING** came along

the hall. A head of wild red hair, a pair of bright brown eyes, and a massive cheeky grin peeked round the door. Lem. Kap came from behind and pushed him. Lem stumbled in and fell over Mum. Her inner self emerged in a sudden sitting up and shouting sort of way.

I quickly clicked on *sign out*. But as I was waved goodbye by **E-SELLALOT**, I noticed that the screen had changed. It had a big message in the centre:

Congratulations!
Your lot is now live on our site!

Oops.

Chapter 12

I must have clicked *continue* by mistake. But I couldn't do anything about it with the boys charging around and waking Mum up.

Much as I'd have loved someone to come and take Granny away – and pay me for it – I didn't really want a long talk from Dad about Why you Really Shouldn't Sell your Grandmother. I decided to come back and take her off when it was more peaceful. If she found out what I'd done, there would be no peace for me – ever.

A GIRL called T.O.M.

I signed out.

'Boys!' warned Mum. She was now standing on one leg with her arms over her head. 'Can't you see I'm trying to do the tree pose?'

'Let's chop the tree down!' said Lem.

'Let's have lunch!' said Mum, before she was forced to do the falling-down tree pose. 'Who wants some chop suey?'

As well as the boys, Mr Truber, aka Mr T, joined us for lunch.

'What happened to your head?' Mr T nodded at Granny's plaster. 'Was it the intruder?'

'No,' said Granny, rubbing the plaster. 'It was Tom. And look what else she did.' She held her hands up, so he could see the plasters on all her fingers.

A GIRL called T.O.M.

'Oh dear, Mrs Fatbottom, you have been in the wars. And how are your knees?'

'They still have plasters on,' I said quickly, before she could show him.

'They are getting better,' said Granny. 'And please call me Geraldine.'

'Thank you. Please call me Lionel.'

Lionel?

'And ℋEAVEN?' asked Mr T, looking at my brother's battered and bruised face. 'That wasn't Tom, was it?'

'No,' said Granny. 'That was a lamppost.'

'Oh dear,' said Mr Truber. A wriggly piece of noodle landed on his plate. 'Boys, stop throwing your chop suey at each other.'

'But he –' began Lem.

'I don't care who started it,' said Mr Truber. 'Just

122

stop.' He nodded his head to make his point. His Mohawk fell off and landed in his chop suey. 'Stop laughing!' he demanded.

But the boys laughed even more. That's because Granny was trying to stick Mr Truber's Mohawk back on his head, but it kept falling off.

'Thank you, Geraldine,' he said, when it had finally stuck. 'I must say, your chop suey is delicious.'

Granny smiled at Mr T. No one told Mr Truber that the chop suey had been cooked long ago. Not even HEAVEN, who is always quick to point things out. In fact, he was being very quiet, staring at the pile of noodles on his plate as if he had great plans for them.

'Has anyone seen my ruby pendant?' asked Mum. 'I'm sure I left it hanging on the hooks in the hall.'

That had to be a motherism. We had so much stuff

on the hooks in the hall there would be no room for a pendant. Everyone shook their heads.

'Jim, how are your plans for your new line in children's parties?' Mr Truber asked Dad.

'Good,' said Dad. 'We're having our first party in the storeroom next Saturday.'

'And who's the lucky kid?' asked Mr Truber. I had a horrible feeling I knew the answer. Because next Saturday was my birthday.

'Tom,' grinned Dad. 'Hers will be our first party. And it's going to be great.' He looked at me with a big, bright smile.

'I can make your costume!' beamed Granny.

'You are so clever, Geraldine,' said Mr Truber, steadying his Mohawk before it fell off again.

'Oh, thank you,' said Granny. 'Would you like to come to Tom's party?'

'I'd be delighted,' said Mr Truber, while I was trying not to choke on my noodles. 'I'll buy a new Mohawk especially for it.'

'And we can try out our new design of **SUPERHERO** party invitations,' said Dad.

'And I'll make lots of interesting and healthy superfood!' said Granny.

I wished I could tell them that I'd much rather have a normal party with normal food, but I was already in enough trouble.

'I think that should do it,' said ℋEAVEN, picking up his plate of noodles and taking it up to his room. I had no idea what he was doing, but knew better than to ask.

Granny started work on my party invitations straight away. First, she made me stand still while she took a photo of me. Then, she told me I had to help her make the invitations on the computer. That was when I found out what Dad's new design for his **SUPERHERO** Party Invitations was.

Each invitation has a **SUPERHERO** on it. Each **SUPERHERO** is doing a **SUPERHERO** pose. Each **SUPERHERO** has his or her head missing. Instead of their head, my head sits on top of their shoulders. My face shows a puzzled expression, as though it's wondering what it's doing there.

All afternoon Granny cackled with delight every time a new invitation came off our printer. All afternoon, I cringed every time a new invitation came off the printer. When we'd finished, Granny told me that I was going to give the invitations out at school on Monday.

Chapter 13

On Monday I went to school with 86 party invitations in my bag. I don't know 86 people. But Granny called Mr Truber and asked him for the names of everyone in my year, plus brothers, sisters, and several teachers. It was a long phone call and included a lot of giggling by Granny.

I handed all my invitations to the bin. I'd tell Granny there was a party on the same day and everyone was going to that one – including me.

Then came lunch.

A GIRL called T.O.M.

I've never had cause to fear my lunchbox. Mum normally does it and, apart from the times it's empty, it's as normal as any other **SUPERHERO** lunchbox. Although, I do remember it was full of washing powder once.

How could I have forgotten that Granny had taken over doing my lunch?

As soon as I undid the clasp (in case you're wondering, it was an Avengers lunchbox, slightly damaged so Dad couldn't sell it in the shop), it sprang open and a tangle of noodles burst out like a mass of pale yellow worms. Granny had filled it with cold chop suey.

I tried to close the lid, but it was too late. Kap and Lem were playing chase – that is, they were running around the hall being chased by a teacher. They passed me just at the wrong moment.

A GIRL called T.O.M.

'Hah, look!' said Kap. 'Tom's got worms for lunch!'
'That's not worms!' said Lem. 'It's the brains of a
monster from outer space!' He swiped my lunchbox
and my chop suey flew out and on to the teacher's
nice clean dress.

'Hah, your guts are coming out!' squealed Kap, then ran off with his brother and an angry teacher chasing them.

Unfortunately, my chop suey troubles didn't end there. When we arrived home, I noticed a sign in Narinda's shop.

Today's special

Homemade Chop Suey

£1.00 per carton

Delicious – made from Granny Fatbottom's own secret recipe

Then there was a notice in Fifi's window.

Special for today only!

Granny Fatbottom's
Food for the soul
All the way from
the Orient!

And in our window? No notice at all. Well, not one about chop suey. But there was one about a special offer on **SUPERHERO** capes – which looked a lot like longyis.

As soon as I was in the flat, I heard tapping coming from the living room.

'Ah, Tom, you're back,' said Granny. 'You can help me put all this on **E-SELLALOT** for your dad.'

I wanted to groan, but instead I smiled sweetly and said I'd love to. It might give me a chance to sneak into my own account and remove her from **E-SELLALOT** before I got into heaps of trouble.

But it was impossible. Despite my assurances that I could manage on my own, Granny insisted on standing over me and giving me advice – which meant yelling out descriptions at me. Such as: **VALUABLE RARE COLLECTOR'S LEGO KEY RING** (It had come free on a cereal packet. Dad had made me take them all off next door's out-of-date stock before they were removed from the shelves.) **LIMITED EDITION WONDER WOMAN FIGURINE** (One of a whole boxful that hadn't sold in the shop.) **RARE 1938 ACTION COMIC – SEE BATMAN'S FIRST EVER STORY!** (Bet you didn't know **BATMAN** was born in a comic in 1938! But this comic was a copy, one of a whole boxful.)

'What's for dinner?' I asked, hoping Granny might go off and cook.

'Chop suey,' she said. 'I just have to heat it up.'

I was mid-groan when a pile of figurines in damaged packaging slid off the table, revealing two larger figurines underneath – the **BATMAN** and **HULK** who live on my shelf. 'Does Dad want to sell these?'

'Of course not,' said Granny. 'We're going to sell them on my **E-SELLALOT** account.'

'But aren't they the ones Dad gave me?'

'You think he will remember?' she laughed.

She had a point. Dad often gives me things he's already given me, especially when he has a boxful. I just put them back in the box when he's not looking. But these were birthday presents and he'd told me they were priceless. Which probably wasn't true, but I still didn't think I should sell them.

'We can see if they really are priceless,' said Granny. 'And you get half the money.'

'Half? But they're mine!'

'But you can't sell them without me.' Yes I can, I thought, but I couldn't tell her that. 'And I need the money towards my next trip,' she added.

'Deal,' I said. If selling **BATMAN** and the **HULK** meant Granny could go on another trip, they certainly were priceless. And, like she said, Dad had probably forgotten all about them. Still, I did feel a twinge of guilt as I put them on **E-SELLALOT** for her.

After that, she made me check the old pyjamas and faded soaps we put up yesterday. There was not a single bid, so Granny went off in a huff to heat up some chop suey.

A GIRL called T.O.M.

I was alone at last.

I logged out of Granny's account. I typed my username, NormalGirl. I'd just tapped in my password *IamSoNormal!!!* when the door flew open and Granny stuck her head in (which no longer has a plaster on it by the way, but her fingers still do). **'TIME FOR DINNER!'** I nearly leapt off the chair.

'Coming,' I said, clicking on *sign out*.

But, as I clicked, I caught a glimpse of my **E-SELLALOT** page.

Congratulations! You have a bid!

Your item will sell!

1 bid - £5.00

Someone out there wanted to buy my grandmother.

Chapter 14

On Tuesday, we walked home with Narinda's mum. I like it when Mrs Singh walks us home, because she always stays a few paces behind so we can talk. But this time we had Elsa with us, who kept laughing when Narinda told her all about the longyis and chop suey for sale in her shop.

When we reached **Pickford Parade**, I stopped dead. There was a giant poster displayed in the window of our shop. A poster inviting the whole world to the shop's first ***SUPERHERO*** party.

A poster with a picture of Spiderman on it – with his head missing. Instead of his head, my confused face.

A GIRL called T.O.M.

Dad's car was parked outside in its usual spot – plastered with smaller versions of the same poster.

'Oh,' said Elsa, looking at Narinda. 'You never said Tom was having a party.'

'Tom never told me,' said Narinda. 'Come on, let's go and listen to some music – we can share my earphones.' She took hold of Elsa's arm and they went into her shop, leaving me standing there. I went into our shop.

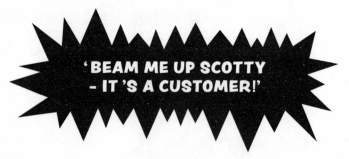

'BEAM ME UP SCOTTY
– IT'S A CUSTOMER!'

'Ah, good, you're back,' said Bilbo, from behind the counter. 'Captain Kirk needs your help. He's on the Bridge.'

A GIRL called T.O.M.

He pointed to the storeroom, which sometimes doubles up as the Bridge of the Starship Enterprise, when it isn't full of boxes.

Dad was tidying up by moving boxes from one side to the other. He was wearing tight black leggings and a wine-coloured long tunic with the Starfleet logo. He was being himself – James Kirk.

Dad got his name because my grandad was very into **STAR TREK** and named him after the first captain of the **STARSHIP ENTERPRISE**. Then Dad changed his surname from Malik to Marvel. So, Dad's name is James Kirk Marvel. Most people call him Jim.

'Hi, Dad,' I said.

'Captain Kirk to you. Did you give all the invitations out?'

'Er, well the thing is –'

A GIRL called T.O.M.

'You didn't give them out,' said Captain Kirk, in the stern voice he uses when the Klingons are causing trouble. 'Mr Truber told Granny he saw you putting them in the bin.'

I waited for him to say something about Why Putting your Party Invitations in the Bin is Wrong, but he didn't. 'But, as it happens, it doesn't matter,' he said instead. 'There's not enough room in here for a party, so we're having it at the Memorial Hall. I'll change the poster in the window and you can give the new invitations out tomorrow. Granny has thought of even more people to invite.'

I imagined the Memorial Hall crammed full with everyone from school, plus a whole load of random people. All of them staring at whatever costume Granny had made for me.

'We can use it to spread the word about the shop

and advertise our new line in children's parties,' said Dad, with the happy face that meant there was no stopping him.

'But – who will look after the shop?' I asked.

'We'll close it and put a notice on the door, directing everyone to the Memorial Hall.' He grabbed my shoulders. 'It's going to be the party to end all parties!'

He looked so happy. How could I tell him I didn't want a party? At least, not one where I had to dress up and pretend to be a **SUPERHERO**, in a costume provided by Granny, who doesn't understand the word *embarrassment*.

I heard a clickety-clack sound coming from the living room. It was a sound I recognised and a sound

A GIRL called T.O.M.

I dreaded. Granny was making something on her sewing machine. That usually meant something for someone to wear. I don't know what is worse – seeing my parents or brother wear something made by Granny or wearing something made by her myself.

As soon as I came in, Granny stopped the sewing machine and threw a longyi over it to hide whatever she was making. 'Ah, Tom, you can tell the computer to behave itself and make new invitations for your party!'

I did my best. I managed to alter the invitations, but I couldn't print them off. It didn't matter how much Granny shouted at me and the computer, the printer wouldn't work.

Even better, when ℋEAVEN came home from school, he refused to fix it. 'I am working on something far more important.' He went straight up to his room.

He stayed in his room until dinner. He sat and smiled at his noodles, which were a bit chewy by now.

Granny was smiling as well. 'I emailed the invitations to Lionel Truber,' she said. 'He's printing them off and he'll give them out tomorrow. So it won't matter if you forget.'

I wasn't smiling.

I lay awake listening to Granny make her Let's Keep Tom Awake noises. I heard the sound of Dad's footsteps coming upstairs, after a long evening of **E-SELLALOT**. I heard him go into the bathroom and come out again. I heard him asking Mum where his Black Panther pyjamas were and heard her angry

A GIRL called T.O.M.

You Woke me Up for That? reply. I heard the sound of **HEAVEN** making calculations in his room while he paced around. Still, I couldn't sleep.

Eventually the flat became quiet, but I was still awake. I decided to make the most of the peace to check on **E-SELLALOT**. I crept downstairs.

Dad's laptop was open on the sofa, showing his **E-SELLALOT** homepage. I logged out and logged in to my own account. My page came up with the only lot I was selling. **One Granny.**

She had a whole page of bids!

Once I was over the shock, I looked carefully. There were three bidders, usernames ***TheGreatest***, ***Bidder007*** and *InnocentMan*.

It looked like they were fighting for her!

The first bidder was ***TheGreatest***, with his bid of £5.00. Then in came *InnocentMan* with a bid of £10. **Bidder007** jumped in with £50 and then the bids kept going up until ***TheGreatest*** stopped bidding, but the other two kept going and now **Bidder007** was winning – with a bid of £5,000!

I heard a creak from upstairs. I logged out of my account and went back into Dad's.

Username ***JKirkM-NCC***.

Password *IAmCaptainKirk!*

Back to his homepage, where he'd left it. A list of what he was selling, next to the list of what he was bidding on. Two things. A rare **HULK** and a rare **BATMAN** figurine. Oh no.

I saw the name of the seller – **ThorasGrannyisGR8.**

Dad was bidding on the figurines that he'd given me for my birthday!

How was I going to –?

That was when I lost consciousness.

A GIRL called T.O.M.

I was lying on the floor, a bright light shining into my eyes and Granny's voice loud in my ear. 'What are you doing down here?'

Then I heard ℋEAVEN. 'Granny, why did you hit Tom over the head with a lightsaber?'

'Lucky it wasn't **THOR'S** hammer,' said Granny, putting the lightsaber down. 'I heard a noise and thought the intruder had come back.'

'What's going on?' Dad came in.

'I was just sneaking down to see whether Granny had any more bids (which she has), when I discovered that you are bidding on the figurines you gave me for my birthday.'

Don't worry, I didn't say that. 'I think I was sleepwalking,' I said.

A GIRL called T.O.M.

On Wednesday, I had a headache, partly from being hit over the head with a lightsaber and partly from 𝒽EAVEN's lecture on how I could be suffering from everything from severe concussion to severe brain abnormality. I decided to go to school, despite my headache – I thought it would be safer. Then Mr Truber handed out Granny's invitations and now everyone wanted to come to my party.

By Thursday, we had 138 people coming to my party. We had run out of chop suey at last, but Granny was now trying out her party food.

'There will be no junk food at Tom's party!' she said, as I looked at my plate of wobbly green jelly, which tasted nothing like Mum's jelly from a packet. 'We are going to have superfoods, fit for **SUPERHEROES**!'

'I like junk food,' I said.

'Bad for you!' hissed Granny. 'I am going to make you all healthy.'

Not if no one eats it, I thought. But I didn't say anything because ℋEAVEN was now giving us a lecture on superfoods.

At lunchtime, I opened my lunchbox without thinking. Bad move.

'Aargh!' Elsa screamed.

Narinda jolted away. 'What is that?'

Everyone was looking at the bright green bogies escaping from my lunchbox.

When I say bright green bogies, I mean the green-dyed cauliflower that we had for dinner last night, to go with the kryptonite jelly. The cauliflower was dyed green because it is better for you than broccoli, and the kryptonite jelly was made out of curly kale. I'd never heard of curly kale before, but I can tell you it doesn't taste very nice. That was Granny's Hulk food. That is, Hulk with a bad cold and no tissues, food.

'This is the food we're having at my party,' I said, loudly. I thought it might put everyone off.

'Yay, party!' yelled Kap as he sped past.

'Great food for a food fight!' yelled Lem, grabbing a piece of green cauliflower and hurling it at Kap.

By the end of school everyone had said they couldn't wait to come to my party. They were going to have a superfood fight fit for a **SUPERHERO** party.

'NUQNEH – GREETINGS,'

said the door, in Klingon and English.

'Ah, Tom, you're back,' said the Klingon behind the counter of our shop. In Klingon.

'Hi, Dad,' I said, in English.

He said something else in Klingon, but I couldn't work it out, apart from the words *Granny, turtle, help,* and *warp drive.*

'Granny wants me to help her put a turtle into warp drive?'

A GIRL called T.O.M.

'No,' Dad sighed. 'I said *plyta*, not *plvghor*! Can't you tell the difference between warp drive and a pizza?'

'Granny wants to send a pizza into warp drive?'

'No,' he sighed. 'Granny wants you to help her make turtle pizza.'

'Is that legal?'

'*Ninja* turtle,' said Dad. 'You didn't think she was going to make pizza out of turtle meat, did you?'

'You didn't say it was a Ninja turtle pizza,' I said.

'Klingons don't have a word for *Ninja*,' he said. 'As you well know.'

I'd had a party before where Mum made a Ninja turtle cake. It had green jelly on it and I was about six. I think I was dressed as a Ninja Turtle at the time, in a costume Granny had made. I seem to remember that my friends loved it a lot more than I did.

A GIRL called T.O.M.

I went up to the flat. When Granny came out of the kitchen wearing a bloodstained apron and wielding a small axe, I knew that this Ninja Turtle pizza wasn't going to be made from jelly.

Granny's turtle was made from wholemeal oat dough topped with vegetables in several shades of green and a sprinkle of chia seeds, which look like fleas.

On Friday at school, I told everyone I'd forgotten my lunchbox. Elsa was sitting with us again and very kindly gave me two carrot sticks and an apple from hers, while she ate her sandwiches, crisps, and cake.

'About your party tomorrow...' said Narinda as we walked home from school behind her mum. 'The thing is, Elsa's asked me to go to the cinema with her. We were going to go in the morning, so we could go to your party, but she's at her dad's this weekend and he can only take us in the afternoon. I don't know what to do now.'

A choice between my party and going to the cinema? I know what I'd do – but Narinda is my best friend and wouldn't dream of letting me down.

'The thing is,' she carried on, 'I promised Elsa I'd go before I knew about your party.' She spoke quietly, looking at the ground, while a funny cold feeling went over me. Then she looked up and her smile was back on. 'If only you'd told me about your plans for a party, I'd have said no to Elsa.'

'I wish I could go to the cinema with you,' I said. Then I saw the look on Narinda's face – like she suddenly had a headache. 'Are you sure you couldn't go another time?'

A GIRL called T.O.M.

'Well, Elsa said she's not too keen on coming to the party, so –'

'You'd rather be with Elsa than at my party.'

'That's not it!' Narinda spoke so quickly I knew it was true. 'I didn't think you'd mind – after all, we are best friends, aren't we?'

I thought we were. But then I thought about how I liked it when we walked home with Narinda's mum or dad, because it meant we walked and chatted. I realised that was the only time we chatted – as soon as we arrived at school, Narinda went off with Elsa.

When Dad gave us a lift, Narinda always sat in the front, leaving me at the back with the boys. When I went to her flat and sat in her room, she was always quiet, but she started chatting when her mum or dad came in.

Narinda was only my friend because her mum and dad said so.

'I thought you were my friend,' I said.

'I am your friend.'

'You're not,' I said. 'You only pretend because of your mum and dad. But I'd rather not have any friends than pretend friends.' We'd reached the shops. 'Goodbye.' I held my head high and walked into our shop.

'TRUTH, JUSTICE, AND A NEW CUSTOMER!'

Dad was behind the counter, dressed as Robin, hunched over his laptop, cloak spilling around him, fingers of one hand tapping furiously, while the other rubbed the band that held his mask. He was on **E-SELLALOT**. He turned his masked eyes towards me as I came in, saw it was me, and closed the screen immediately. But I'd already seen what he was doing – bidding on **BATMAN** and **HULK**.

'Ah, hello, Tom,' he said. He spoke with an American accent that didn't sound anything like Robin. 'Bet you can't wait for tomorrow and the most amazing party ever. Do you know how many are coming? 235! And that's without the ones who will just turn up.'

233, I thought, as Narinda and Elsa wouldn't be there.

'Yeah, great.' I trudged upstairs.

It was strangely quiet in the flat. The kitchen door was shut and had a note stuck to it.

A GIRL called T.O.M.

> Dear Heaven,
>
> Spiderman Pizza ready to go in oven. Please set the timer so it is cooked perfectly for dinner.
>
> From your loving Granny.

I went upstairs to check on poor **Mr Prickles**. He was looking very sad in his pot without his arm. His poor arm was sticking out from its little pot as though reaching for **Mr Prickles**.

'I know how you feel,' I said. 'I've lost my best friend as well.'

We had Granny's Spiderman pizza for dinner. I think his mask was made from chopped liver, the web from cottage cheese, his hidden eyes from beetroot. HEAVEN remarked on how many superfoods it contained and what each one does to you. By the time he'd finished I was ready to live to 132, while my heart slowed down so much it stopped beating.

When Mum said I didn't have to help wash up because it was my birthday tomorrow, I was very glad to go. But I did wonder why she shut the door firmly behind me and why there was a hum of hushed conversation as soon as they thought I'd gone.

I went into the living room. Granny's sewing machine rose from a sea of bits of cut and torn cloth on the desk next to the computer, but there was no sign of what she'd been making.

I logged into Granny's **E-SELLALOT** account. The

bids on my **BATMAN** and **HULK** figurines were up to £150 each. The high bidder was *JkirkM-NCC* – aka my dad.

I went into my own account and put bids of £250 on each. He'd never go higher than that. I'd win them and Dad would never know he'd been bidding on something he'd given me. Then I checked the one item I had for sale.

The bids on Granny had gone up to £10,000. ***Bidder007*** was still the current high bidder.

Who was ***Bidder007***? Who was willing to pay so much for her?

I'd find out tomorrow.

Chapter 15

'THE ENTERPRISE
HAS A BIRTHDAY GIRL!
WAKE UP AND PARTY!'

HEAVEN must have changed the message on my alarm clock. I knew better than to try and turn it off.

'HAPPY BIRTHDAY, TOM-TOM GIRL!'

Granny peered over my bunk and thrust a shiny gold package at me. My alarm clock remained quiet.

A GIRL called T.O.M.

I opened my present. It was a longyi, bright green with a bold pattern in a deep shade of bogey. It was the worst longyi I'd seen so far, but I thought I'd better wear it.

By the time I came down in my terrible new longyi, there was smoke everywhere and ꟼHEAVEN was overriding the smoke alarm.

'They ought to invent a smoke alarm that can tell the difference between Granny's cooking and fire-smoke,' he said. 'Happy birthday. What on earth are you wearing?' He looked down at my longyi. Even ꟼHEAVEN thought it was awful.

I went into the kitchen to investigate what Granny was burning for breakfast. She'd made super-muesli.

'No sugar in this!' she said. 'Just superfood!' She gave me a bowl of smoking nuts and dried up fruit, sprinkled with chia seeds. 'Why are you wearing the tablecloth I gave you?' She looked down at my longyi.

'I –' But Granny was laughing so much I couldn't be heard. By the time she'd managed to explain what was so funny, she had hiccups as well.

A GIRL called T.O.M.

Apparently the patterns on what I thought was a longyi are supposed to be cacti. She'd bought the tablecloth for me in Pemandagan because she knows how much I like my cactus – the one she tried to kill.

'Oh, lovely, you've made a special birthday breakfast.' Mum came in, wearing her Captain Marvel pyjamas. 'Happy birthday, Tom!'

'Happy birthday,' yawned Dad, as he came in wearing his Black Panther pyjamas.

'Time to open your presents!' Granny leapt up and opened a cupboard, spilling shiny wrapped packages.

I opened my presents. This is what I got:

 A longyi (a real one, not a tablecloth) and shiny shirt from Granny.

A longyi and shiny shirt from Mum and Dad.

A box of wires from 𝓗EAVEN, which he

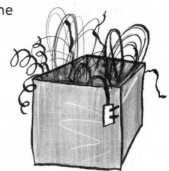

snatched off me as soon as I'd opened it. This is normal behaviour from 𝓗EAVEN on my birthday.

A packet of edible seeds from Granny.

A packet of nuts from Granny.

'Thank you – it's all lovely,' I said.

'You don't think that's all, do you?' laughed Granny. 'You haven't had your main present yet!'

We had to move to the living room for the

A GIRL called T.O.M.

Opening of The Main Present. Correction – two main presents. Two identical large boxes wrapped in gold paper, like a pair of coffins.

I took the wrapping off Coffin Number One. It revealed a golden box. Granny stood with her hands clasped in front of her, eager grin on her face. I lifted the lid.

You really don't want to know what was in there.

'It's from all of us,' said Granny. 'But it was my idea. And I made it.'

'You made this?' I asked.

'Of course! Why do you think I've been too busy to collect you from school?'

I suppose I'd better tell you what was in that box.

It looked like Frankenstein had decided to make a cuddly toy version of his monster, using fish and vegetables instead of bits of people. The head was a giant soft pomegranate and, instead of hair, it had wavy green wool that was supposed to look like curly kale. For eyes it had two big sprouts and I think the nose was supposed to look like a beetroot. Its body was a giant purple aubergine, the arms massive sardines, and the legs were giant mackerels. The feet looked like sweet potatoes.

'It's, um, lovely?' I squeaked. 'But it's too big to go in my room.'

'It's not for our room!' laughed Granny, lifting it up, making the sardine arms flap. She turned it round, revealing a large red zip down the back. 'It's your party costume! You're going as the Superfood Girls, bringing health to all who touch you.'

SUPERFOOD GIRLS?

That's when I guessed what was in the second box. I looked at it, trying hard not to cry.

'I told you she'd like it!' Granny wrapped her arms round me. 'Look, she's overcome and nearly crying with happiness! Now, open the other one.'

As I'd feared, the second box contained an almost identical Superfood Fish and Vegetable Monster costume. Which could only mean one thing – Granny was going to be the second SUPERFOOD GIRL.

But I was wrong.

167

A GIRL called T.O.M.

'This one's for Narinda!' squealed Granny, bouncing up and down with excitement. 'She knows all about it and kept it secret!'

No wonder Narinda didn't want to come to my party. But why hadn't she told me?

Because she wasn't my friend, that's why.

Mum looked at her watch. 'Tom, you'd better take them round to Narinda's now. Give us time to get everything ready for the party.'

'But –' I couldn't go to Narinda's. 'Why don't I help?'

'No, no,' said Granny. 'You can't stay here – then it won't be a surprise for you, will it?'

I wished I could tell them that I'd had enough of surprises.

Chapter 16

Granny took me along the walkway at the back of our flats to Narinda's. I thought about running down the stairs opposite her back door and escaping along the alley behind our shops. But I was carrying a large gold box containing one Superfood costume, while Granny could barely be seen behind the other.

Mr Singh opened the door. 'Happy birthday, Tom!' he grinned. 'Here, let me take that.' He took the box from Granny, so she could hurry back to our flat to continue with The Preparations for Tom's

A GIRL called T.O.M.

Party. Meanwhile, I had no choice but to go into Narinda's.

Her dad left us in her bedroom, staring down at the two gold boxes on her bed. 'Why didn't you tell me?' I said.

'I didn't know how to.'

'Because you're not my friend?'

'Of course I'm your friend. Your granny made me keep it a secret, but I had to try on these costumes to make sure they fit. You should have seen me – I looked –'

I tried to imagine Narinda with a pomegranate head, fish arms and legs, and aubergine body. I couldn't help it – I grinned. 'You must have looked funny.'

Narinda grinned back. 'I looked really stupid.' She laughed. I laughed. We both stood there laughing at each other – and then we stopped.

'It's not funny,' said Narinda.

'No, it isn't,' I said. 'But at least you can go to the cinema with Elsa instead.'

'I've been thinking about that,' she said. 'I can't let you go alone to a party looking like that.'

'I could tell my mum and dad that you're not well,' I said.

'But my mum and dad will tell them I'm fine,' said Narinda.

'I'll tell them we're not friends any more. Then they can't make you go.'

'But we are friends!'

'Really?'

'Really,' she said.

'Friends enough to wear a Superfood Fish and Vegetable Monster costume?'

A GIRL called T.O.M.

She looked at me like she had the worst headache ever. 'I think so,' she squeaked.

There was a **THUMP-THUMP-THUMP** up the stairs, **tramp-tramp-tramp** along the hallway. **'Kabam!!'** A shout as Narinda's door burst open and in came a **SPIDERMAN** twin, complete with mask that bulged with the hair trying to stay under it. **'Kaboom!'** Followed by an identical **SPIDERMAN**. 'We're dressed and ready for your party!' they shouted together.

'You're taking us to the party!' said Spiderman 1.

'Because Mum has to stay in the shop!' said Spiderman 2.

'What's in these boxes?' They flung off the lids. 'Wow, the coolest thing ever!' They grabbed a Superfood Fish and Vegetable Monster each.

A GIRL called T.O.M.

'Hey, mine's got a zip at the back!' said **SPIDERMAN** 1.

'So has mine!' said **SPIDERMAN** 2.

'These are way cooler than **SPIDERMAN**!' Before we knew it, both boys were trying to climb into the Superfood Monsters. Narinda and I jumped up and helped them, pulling the zips right up to their pomegranate heads.

'Mmmmffff!' said Superfood Fish and Vegetable Monster 1.

'Mmmmffff!' said Superfood Fish and Vegetable Monster 2.

Narinda and I looked at each other.

'I've got an idea,' we both said together.

Chapter 17

It really was the most spectacular **SUPERHERO** party Pickford had ever witnessed. Granny was dressed as a Ninja Turtle, Mum was Cat Woman, HEAVEN was a two-headed, eight-legged monster from some

A GIRL called T.O.M.

obscure comic book, and Dad was Captain Kirk. Nearly everyone from my school turned up dressed as their favourite **SUPERHEROES**, including several of Dad's customers and Mr Truber as Mr T with his new Mohawk. There was someone from the local radio there and someone from the local news-blog was taking pictures of the incredible **SUPERFOOD GIRLS** who'd come to save the world from chips, tomato sauce, and fizzy drinks.

A GIRL called T.O.M.

A fashion designer wanted a closer look at their costumes, but couldn't catch them. A slim **SPIDERMAN** wore dark glasses. Another Spiderman had a wizard's beard. Sergeant Ben and PC Meer were keeping order dressed as RoboCops, preventing any food fights. The adults ate the food, as soon as the woman from the local news-blog had taken pictures of it.

But the best thing about it was that I wasn't there. I'd been to the cinema and now I was in a café with Narinda and Elsa, eating chips with tomato sauce and a fizzy drink. I was wearing jeans and a top borrowed from Narinda. I was being normal and it was brilliant.

Lem and Kap had been thrilled to wear the **SUPERHERO** Fish and Vegetable costumes. We told Narinda's parents that the twins were going to the party with my parents. My parents thought they were going with Narinda and me. All we had to do was hide while the boys went off to the party in our costumes, then sneak out the back way to meet Elsa when her dad came to pick us up.

Simple and brilliant. What could possibly go wrong?

Nothing.

Until Elsa's dad was driving us home with the local radio on and he turned the volume up to hear the news.

'AND NOW OVER TO OUR REPORTER WHO HAS BEEN ENJOYING HIMSELF AT THE *SUPERHERO* PARTY AT PICKFORD MEMORIAL HALL,' ANNOUNCED THE RADIO. 'WHERE MEN, WOMEN, AND CHILDREN HAVE BEEN SHOWING OFF THEIR *SUPERHERO* COSTUMES. WE'VE HAD EVERYTHING FROM IRONMAN, TO SUPERMAN AND

BATMAN, EVERY ALIEN IMAGINABLE INCLUDING ONE WITH EIGHT ARMS AND TWO HEADS, THE CRAZIEST NINJA TURTLE EVER SEEN, AND THE TWO SUPERFOOD KIDS DRESSED IN WHAT CAN ONLY BE DESCRIBED AS A FISH AND VEGETABLE MONSTER MASH-UP, WHICH HAS CAUGHT THE ATTENTION OF A FASHION DESIGNER. OVER TO YOU, JUSTIN. JUSTIN?'

It went all crackly for a moment, then Justin the reporter spoke. **'BREAKING NEWS!** THERE HAS BEEN A SERIOUS INCIDENT HERE AT THE PARTY. THE SUPERFOOD FISH AND VEGETABLE COSTUMES HAVE BEEN FOUND EMPTY, BUT THERE IS NO SIGN OF THE TWO GIRLS WHO WERE WEARING THEM. THE TWO ROBOCOPS HAVE CALLED FOR BACK-UP. THERE IS A RUMOUR THAT THE GIRLS HAVE BEEN ABDUCTED BY ALIENS, BUT WE CAN'T CONFIRM THAT - AS FAR AS WE KNOW, ALL THE ALIENS AT THE PARTY HAVE BEEN

178

ACCOUNTED FOR. BACK TO THE STUDIO. '

'Is that the party you didn't want to go to, Elsa?' said her dad. 'Don't blame you.'

Elsa shrugged. I looked at Narinda, who was looking at me.

'I think we'd better go to the Memorial Hall,' said Narinda.

'Where have you been?' demanded Captain Kirk, aka Dad. 'We thought the Klingons had got you.'

I'd asked Elsa's dad to drop us off round the corner, so we could sneak in and pretend we'd been there all the time. But Captain Kirk was outside the Memorial Hall, standing by a police car with blue flashing lights. Next to the car, speaking into a police radio, was PC RoboCop Meer.

A GIRL called T.O.M.

'Cancel that, we've found the girls.' RoboCop Meer clicked off the radio. 'You'd better go inside.' We went inside the hall, where the very first person we saw was Cat Woman, aka Mum, doing the tree pose and chanting *oooooooohhhhhhhhhmmmmm!*

'You can stop trying to calm yourself,' said Captain Kirk. 'We've found them.'

Mum came out of her tree pose. I waited for the inner dragon, but I got a tearful mum who held me tight. 'You gave us a fright,' she said. 'And we didn't know how we were going to tell Narinda's mum and dad. Thank goodness we won't have to now.'

'THORA, MY DARLING TOM-TOM GIRL!'
Granny did her best to charge towards me in her Ninja Turtle costume. She looked like a waddling giant green cuddly-toy pizza with

A GIRL called T.O.M.

little green wrinkled legs.

'Mmmfff!' I said, as she swamped me in a big, soft hug.

'I knew it,' said the two-headed, eight-legged monster behind her, aka ℋEAVEN. 'Thora, why do you always have to bring attention to yourself?' He used two of his eight hands to adjust his second head. 'Honestly, look at you!'

I looked down at myself. I was wearing jeans and a top, next to my best friend who was wearing jeans and a top. I looked at my family – Captain Kirk in his smart uniform, Cat Woman beside him, Granny the Turtle and ℋEAVEN, who was now explaining the finer points of how to manage two heads to a couple of boys from my class, who were both dressed as Ironman.

I looked around the hall, where my party was buzzing. I saw a banner over the stage -

Happy Birthday Super Tom-Tom

I looked at the floor. 'I'm sorry,' I said. 'The thing is –' How could I tell them that I didn't want this **SUPERHERO** party? 'The thing is –'

'We got hot,' said Narinda. 'Those costumes were really hot to wear. We had to cool off.'

'Oh dear,' said Dad. 'We should have thought of that.'

'I may have underestimated the level of activity you girls would indulge in,' said HEAVEN. 'Thereby creating far more heat than expected.'

'Yes,' said Mum. 'You were both very energetic.'

'We were trying to show how healthy we were,' said Narinda.

'So, where did you get to?' asked Mum. 'We looked everywhere for you – it was time to cut your cake.'

'We went out for some fresh air,' said Narinda.

'Sorry,' I said. Then I had a horrible thought. 'Um – where are the twins?'

'You mean **SPIDERMAN** 1 and 2,' said Dad. 'They've been causing trouble ever since we found your empty costumes. They were fine until then.'

The twins had obviously taken off their Superfood costumes and were now causing trouble in the **SPIDERMAN** costumes they wore underneath. I spotted a **SPIDERMAN** chasing another

A GIRL called T.O.M.

SPIDERMAN. As they came charging towards us, I saw curls of red hair escaping from their masks.

'Careful!' warned Dad, as they nearly crashed into him. 'Watch out!'

'You can have your Superfood costumes back!' said Spiderman 1.

'They were far too hot so we took them off!' yelled Spiderman 2.

'What did you say?' said Dad. Then he turned to me with his stern Captain Kirk look.

Chapter 18

The party was over and I was in the living room having the biggest talk ever about Being Grateful. It was delivered by a very stressed Captain Kirk, with a Ninja Turtle hovering in the background. He said *and another thing* five times, *and what's more* four times, and *have you any idea?* six times.

'Sorry I didn't want to wear Granny's Fish and Vegetable costume,' I said.

'But why not?' demanded the Ninja Turtle.

BECAUSE I WANT TO BE NORMAL!!!!!

But I didn't say that. I looked at my dad and tried to imagine him collecting us from school dressed like the other dads, but I couldn't. I tried to imagine him driving a normal car, but I couldn't.

My dad belonged in his shop. He belonged in his **SUPERHERO** car and his **SUPERHERO** costumes. I couldn't imagine him being any different.

I looked at Granny in her Ninja Turtle costume that she must have spent ages making. The costumes she made for Narinda and me that the radio presenter had called Monster mash-ups must have been a lot of hard work. I thought of all the time she'd spent in the kitchen, cooking. She'd done all this for me.

'WARNING!
OUTER DEFENCES BREACHED!'

A GIRL called **T.O.M.**

We all jumped. But it was only the doorbell for the back door to our flat. **HEAVEN** changed it some time ago, but most people just knock.

'Can you see who that is?' said Dad. 'I need to check something on **E-SELLALOT**.'

I went down the hall and opened our back door. And there stood a slender man dressed in a smart suit and dark glasses, holding a briefcase. I couldn't tell whether he recognised me, but I certainly recognised him. What was he doing here?

'You are **NormalGirl**,' he said. 'From **E-SELLALOT**.'

A GIRL called T.O.M.

I could only nod.

'I am **InnocentMan** and I have come to collect One Granny, Old but Good Condition.'

My mouth fell open.

'You will find payment in here.' He tapped his briefcase. '£15,000 in used bank notes, guaranteed untraceable.'

My mouth refused to close.

'Who is it?' Mum called from the kitchen.

'Um, it's someone for Granny,' I said.

Mum came down the hall in her Cat Woman suit. 'How nice to meet you,' she said. 'Do come in and I'll tell my mother you're here.' She took him into the living room, where Captain Kirk was frowning at the computer. 'Jim, someone here for Mum.'

Dad turned round, still frowning. Then he saw **InnocentMan**. 'Oh, hello, you're the man who bought all the power gems. I didn't know you knew my mother-in-law.'

InnocentMan didn't reply.

'Tom, go and fetch Granny,' said Mum. 'Oh, here she is.'

Granny the Turtle waddled in, minus head. I mean, minus the turtle head. Granny's own head was sticking up from the Turtle costume. 'Who are you?' She peered at **InnocentMan**.

'You were at the party.' HEAVEN came in wearing his monster costume, but with one head – his own. 'I recognise the shades, which you wore over your Spiderman mask.'

InnocentMan ignored him. 'The Turtle comes with me,' he said, landing his briefcase on the floor with a thump.

'What are you talking –?' Dad began.

'I'll get it!' ♀HEAVEN ran to the back door.

'Two visitors in the same afternoon,' smiled Mum. 'I'd better put the kettle on.'

'Here we are.' ♀HEAVEN came into the living room – with a man wearing a longyi and a wizard beard. 'This gentleman says he's known to someone here as **Bidder007** from **E-SELLALOT**? Does anyone –?'

'Hah!' The new visitor, aka **Bidder007**, didn't wait for ♀HEAVEN to finish. **'Got you!'** he pointed at *InnocentMan*. **'Caught in the act! Hand it over, now!'**

'Do you two know each other?' asked Mum. 'Would you like a cup of tea?'

'Yes and no,' said **Bidder007**. 'Yes, I know this man. He is a thief and smuggler of rare stolen gems from Pemandagan. But no, I don't drink tea, only coffee.'

'You are mistaken,' said *InnocentMan*.

'I am not. I haven't drunk tea since it brought me out in spots when I was a child.' He pointed at *InnocentMan*. 'And you are **BANE EGO,** the infamous thief and smuggler, one of the most dangerous criminals the world has known. I'd recognise those dark glasses anywhere. And you've been –'

'WARNING! OUTER DEFENCES BREACHED!'

A GIRL called T.O.M.

'Another visitor?' said Mum, as **HEAVEN** went to answer the door.

'*I AM NOT STAYING,*' growled *InnocentMan*, aka **BANE EGO**, the world's most dangerous criminal. Then he made a grab for Granny. I thought he was going to strangle her, which would have been very unfair, as she'd been standing there quietly for a change.

But he didn't strangle her. He grabbed the cheap chain from her neck, twisting his fist until it snapped, and ran out of the living room, with the chain dangling and the ruby clenched in his fist. It was so quick that Granny didn't have time to protest.

YOU – SHALL – NOT – PASS!!

Gandalf roared from the hallway.

'NOT NOW, GANDALF,' I heard ***InnocentMan*** snap. 'I'm trying to escape with a priceless ruby – have you any idea how hard it was to –?'

'Stay where you are!' I heard **HEAVEN** booming down the hall. 'You may call yourself Innocent Man, but our new visitors know that you are quite the opposite. They are a team of agents from Pemandagan. Their colleague, Agent U, is already here. We know him as ***Bidder007***.'

A GIRL called T.O.M.

'More visitors?' wailed Mum. 'I'll need a bigger kettle!'

'No need for tea,' said **Bidder007,** aka Agent U. 'My back-up team have arrived to arrest **BANE EGO**. But I shall return, to discuss your reward.'

A GIRL called T.O.M.

He ran out. We crowded into the living room doorway, to watch **BANE EGO** being taken down by a team of agents in longyis and false beards. This involved knocking over most of the boxes stacked up in our hallway.

OOOF!

Chapter 19

'Are you sure you won't have some tea?' said Mum later that evening, as we sat round the table with Agent U. 'Or I could run next door for some coffee – I'm sure Mrs Singh will open the shop for me.'

'No thank you,' said Agent U. He'd come back to thank us for helping him. He told us that he worked for the Pemandagan government, tracking down a priceless ruby that had been stolen and smuggled out of the country. That was why he disguised himself with a false beard and moustache.

A GIRL called T.O.M.

The thieves had hidden the ruby by putting it on a cheap chain and hanging it right at the back of a rack of plastic rubies on a market stall in Pemandagan.

They hadn't expected Granny to come along and buy all the rubies, including the real one.

BANE EGO was the leader of the gang. He followed Granny and tracked her down to our shop. That's why he followed me home from school and pretended to bump into me when the twins were fighting – so he could snatch the ruby from round my neck. He did the same to **HEAVEN**.

He managed to buy all the rubies from our shops, apart from two – the one that Mum hung on the hooks in the hall, and the one Granny wore around her neck.

The one she was wearing when I took her photo for **E-SELLALOT**.

A GIRL called T.O.M.

'BANE EGO broke into your flat,' said Agent U. 'But he only managed to take the ruby hanging on the hook in the hall before Gandalf and the HULK got the better of him. Then I saw the ruby on E-SELLALOT – when I was looking for a longyi. But BANE EGO saw the ruby as well and, after bidding against him for a while, I decided to let him buy it, so I could catch him – and it worked.' He looked at Granny's ruby, which was sitting in the middle of the table. 'Of course, I will have to make sure it is the real one, before we release your reward.'

'You saw the ruby on E-SELLALOT?' frowned Dad.

'Reward?' said Granny.

'REWARD?' I said, loudly, to distract Dad from thinking about how the ruby had really ended up on E-SELLALOT.

'Once I've tested the ruby.' Agent U opened the small case he'd brought with him. He took out a pair of fine tweezers and used them to take Granny's ruby off the chain. Then he rubbed it in a small soft cloth and held it to the light. 'So far so good,' he said.

'He's checking the colour,' said ƼHEAVEN.

Agent U then put a magnifying glass in his eye and held the ruby up to inspect it.

'He's checking for flaws,' said ƼHEAVEN. 'It should have some, whereas a fake ruby will be completely smooth.'

Agent U put his magnifying glass down. 'All in order,' he said. He took a thin piece of metal out of his case and scratched the ruby with it.

'It shouldn't scratch,' said ƼHEAVEN. 'Only another ruby can scratch a ruby.'

A GIRL called T.O.M.

We watched as Agent U took a small piece of smooth glass from his case. He scratched the ruby against it. 'Perfect,' he said, looking at the thin line the ruby had made.

'A ruby will scratch glass,' said 𝒽EAVEN.

'One final test,' said Agent U.

'I trust you mean the lemon juice test?' said 𝒽EAVEN. 'To see whether it will go cloudy if dropped in.'

'Oh, I think we're out of lemon juice,' said Mum. 'I could pop next door and get some?'

'No need,' said Agent U. 'I have my own supply.' He brought out a small glass jar full of liquid. He unscrewed the top and dropped the ruby in.

'Professional jewellers' cleaning fluid,' said 𝒽EAVEN. 'It contains a carboxylic acid, as does lemon juice. It will damage a fake.'

A GIRL called T.O.M.

'Very good,' said Agent U. 'Are you considering a career in rare gems?'

'Oh no,' said HEAVEN. 'My talents lie elsewhere.'

Agent U lifted the ruby out of the fluid with a pair of tweezers, dried it in the cloth, and held it to the light. 'A very large, very rare, very perfect ruby. It's priceless.'

A GIRL called T.O.M.

'And you found it on **E-SELLALOT**?' asked Dad.
'From a seller called NormalGirl?' I began to squirm.

'Not the ruby as such,' said Agent U. 'It was –'

Beeep! Dad's **E-SELLALOT** alarm went off in his pocket. That meant something he was bidding on was about to finish. 'Excuse me.' He dashed off into the living room.

'I must now go back and discuss your reward with my embassy,' said Agent U.

Mum showed him out. 'He didn't even have tea,' she said, slumping at the table. 'What a day.'

A shout came from the living room. '**Yess!!!**' That was Dad's triumphant **E-SELLALOT** shout. '**Take that, NormalGirl!**' Followed by a long silence.

Dad came into the kitchen, looking like Captain Kirk had just realised that the **STARSHIP ENTERPRISE** was surrounded by

A GIRL called T.O.M.

Klingons. 'I've just paid a lot of money for two rare collectible figurines,' he said. 'A **BATMAN** and a **HULK**. I had to outbid someone with the username NormalGirl, which is beginning to sound familiar. They were listed by someone with the username **THORASGRANNYISGR8**. I've just checked the address to pick them up from, and it's *Granny Fatbottom's Emporium of Delights, Superhero, Pickford Parade, Pickford.*'

'I'll fetch them!' Granny ran upstairs.

Dad turned his stern Captain Kirk face to me. 'Are you NormalGirl?'

I nodded down at the table.

'Oh dear,' said Mum. 'I'd better go down and check the shop.' She often says this when I'm about to have a Good Talking To.

A GIRL called T.O.M.

'Why did you want to sell the figurines I gave you?' demanded Dad. 'And, could you explain the item you'd listed on **E-SELLALOT**? One Granny, old but –'

'Here they are!' Granny burst in, **BATMAN** in one hand, **HULK** in the other. 'Pay up!'

'Technically, he can't do that,' said ℋEAVEN. 'As they were not your figurines to sell.'

'BUT I SOLD THEM FOR TOM!' protested Granny. **'AND WE SHARE THE PROFIT!'**

'Did you agree to this, Tom?' Dad folded his arms at me.

'Well –' But I had no excuse.

'I expect you needed the space, as you have lost half of your room now.' Dad looked at Granny. 'And ℋEAVEN is right. You really shouldn't have talked Tom into selling them.'

'I'll get it!' Granny rushed to the door.

'WARNING!
OUTER DEFENCES BREACHED!'

'I've come to see NormalGirl.' I heard a familiar voice. 'From E-SELLALOT. I'm *TheGreatest*. I was bidding on something very important to me. I hope I'm not too late.'

'Oh, Lionel,' giggled Granny. 'Do come in.'

TheGreatest was Mr Truber!

Chapter 20

Granny led Mr Truber into the kitchen by the hand. 'Lionel.' She looked up at him with a crazy grin.

'Geraldine.' Mr Truber looked down at her, with a crazy grin of his own. 'I'm so glad you are still here – I was worried you'd have been taken away by now.'

'Taken away?' protested Granny. 'I am completely innocent! I didn't know the ruby was real!'

'What ruby?' said Mr Truber.

'The one that my grandmother was wearing around her neck,' said HEAVEN. 'When TOM took her picture in an attempt to sell her on **E-SELLALOT**. Which, as well as being illegal, inadvertently caused –'

'But, Geraldine!' exclaimed Mr Truber. 'You are far more priceless to me than all the precious rubies in the world! I should have told you how I feel about you sooner – but I can't bear the thought of anyone else taking you away.'

Granny's face did something very odd. It sort of closed in on itself while her eyes went big and her eyelashes went all fluttery. 'Oh, Lionel! No one is taking me away. The other two bidders only wanted the ruby.'

'They are fools,' said Mr Truber. 'Geraldine.' He made a face as silly as Granny's. 'Will you come and live with me?'

'Of course I will!' said Granny. 'Can I come right now? I've been sharing a room with Tom and you wouldn't believe what I've had to put up with!' She ran upstairs. 'I'll pack right away!'

'I'll help!' Mr Truber went up after her.

Dad gave me a long talk about How it is Rude to Sell Your Grandmother. It contained the phrases *after all she's done for you* and *have you any idea how hard she worked for your party?* It contained a lot of head shaking. But it also had a twitch at the corner of his mouth. One which made my own mouth twitch as I tried not to grin.

A GIRL called T.O.M.

'It's really not funny,' he said, trying so hard to be stern that it was very hard not to laugh. 'And, as HEAVEN pointed out, not very legal. Even though things worked out well in the end, it was – Tom, will you please at least try not to laugh while I'm telling you off!'

That did it. We both started laughing hysterically.

'What's so funny?' Mum came up from checking the shop, carrying a box. 'I thought you were having a stern word with Tom about trying to sell my mother. Even if things did work out well and the shop is no longer in danger, thanks to the reward.' She put the box on the table. 'This was on the counter in the shop – it must have arrived earlier.'

'It's for Tom.' Dad picked up the box. 'Sorry it's a little late, but the bidding on E-SELLALOT only finished yesterday, so I couldn't get it any sooner.

A GIRL called T.O.M.

Happy birthday.' He handed me the box. 'It's something to add to your little collection.'

I prepared to put on my most grateful face for whatever was in the box – and I made a promise to myself that I would make sure Granny never tried to sell it. I didn't try to guess which **SUPERHERO** figurine it would be – you never know with Dad.

But it wasn't a figurine. It wasn't even **SUPERHERO** related.

It was another box. A smooth white cardboard box, with a clear panel at the front. And, sitting on the other side of the panel, in a smart pot, was a beautiful little cactus.